SWEET & WILD

SWEET & WILD

ALEX LARKSPUR

CONTENT WARNINGS

- Insects, specifically bees
- Death of a parent to illness
- Injury to throat
- Violence
- Mob Violence
- Violent death of animals
- Abusive/toxic relationship
- Debt and money issues
- Illness of a sibling
- House Fire
- Implied sex scenes

To everyone who has needed a soft place to land

1

THE FOREST

THE TREES WELCOMED MICAH HARLOW LIKE AN OLD FRIEND even though he had never been in this particular forest. It had been a rainy few days, but the spring morning was finally crisp and cool, not a sweaty, unforgiving, humid monstrosity. Instead, it was a perfect day for foraging. Micah stepped carefully through the trees, humming to himself, avoiding mud puddles as best he could. As he leapt from one root to the next, his worn leather satchel bounced on his hip and the milk bottle in his carry basket fell over. He took a moment to right the bottle—luckily none had spilled—and continued his search.

Sun dappled between the oak leaves and danced on the ground. Birds twittered around him, filling the morning air with their songs. He could hear animals scampering through the underbrush. He straightened his wide-brimmed straw hat and pushed up his sleeves. A grin spread across his freckled face when he spotted exactly what he was looking for.

Every forest, whatever its size, has its guardian spirit. And the forest outside of Roseyard was anything but small. Micah's mother had always taught him that before taking anything from the forest, you should make an offering to its spirit. They did it every week when she was still alive, back in Steephall, where the woods were considerably

"

smaller than here. There might be a more established altar somewhere in the Roseyard Woods, but the small outcropping of rocks here was perfect for now.

Micah knelt, not caring at all about the mud. He arranged the stones to be a bit more uniform, then reached into his bag, retrieving sprigs of dried heather, a piece of flint, and his beeswax candle. He placed the heather at the edges of the makeshift altar, then set the candle on the stone he had placed in the center. He retrieved the bottle of milk from his basket, along with the two best rolls of fine bread from yesterday's batch, three chicken eggs, and a yellow ribbon. Sometimes, the guardians liked pretty things as well as food, and he had little use for it. After he set the last of his offerings down, he struck the flint and lit the candle.

Micah breathed in beeswax with a hint of smoke for a moment before saying softly, "Whatever spirit may guard this forest, I offer these gifts to you in exchange for the bounty of the woods. I will take no more than I need, and I will leave the forest in peace."

The birdsong stopped for just a moment before picking up again in earnest. Closing his eyes, Micah rose. He'd come back for the empty bottle later. Sure that his offering was enough, he turned, took a breath, opened his eyes, and walked away.

Ten paces later, he heard a twig snap. He spun around and saw a man partially obscured by the trees. He was at least a head taller than Micah, probably a few years older too. He had tanned skin, dark, shaggy hair that trailed to his shoulders, and a surprisingly well-kept beard. His shirt and pants were tattered and covered in dirt, as if he had been living out in the woods for quite some time. The man's bare feet were dirty, but surprisingly not caked in mud. His eyes were a deep, dark green and they looked wild even with the good-natured smile on his face.

"Hello," the man said, his voice a deep rumble.

"Good morning," Micah replied, his face heating in embarrassment. The man had probably been watching the entire time he set up the altar and said his little prayer.

The man stepped forward and Micah found himself rooted to the spot. He couldn't pull his eyes away from the man; it was a truly otherworldly sight. The stranger's steps made no sound, but he walked with great weight and purpose, as though a tree had suddenly uprooted itself and journeyed through the forest.

Micah hardly had time to breathe before the man was upon him, standing mere inches away. He looked Micah up and down, then plucked the hat from Micah's head. He reached out, taking a short, dirty-blond curl between his fingers, pulling it softly before dropping it, and then examined the hat, turning it over and running his fingers across the petals of the flowers laced through its straw. He placed the hat back on Micah's head and smiled at him.

"What's your name?" he asked, his deep voice resonating in Micah's chest.

"Micah," Micah said, voice softer than he meant it to be. "Micah Harlow, sir."

"Haven't seen you around before," he said, looking at the embroidered collar of Micah's shirt. He pinched it between his fingers and pulled it, and Micah, closer.

"I just moved to Roseyard about a month ago," Micah said, and with a quick nervous smile added, "First time coming into the forest."

"Mmm," the man said, the rumble of his voice lifting the hair on the back of Micah's neck.

Micah swallowed, frozen in the presence of this man. Now that he was closer, he could smell him, a deep, earthy scent mixed with the sharp tang of pine needles. It wasn't unpleasant. Micah's gaze drifted to the man's face, mere inches from his own, those wild green eyes still studiously examining the design around Micah's neck. Then he noticed the man's unusually long, sharply pointed ears. And how had he not spotted the two short antlers, like those of a young stag, growing from under the thick tresses? Oh. *Oh.* Heart racing, Micah ran through their conversation thus far and determined that he had been extremely polite. Good.

The man dropped the collar suddenly and glanced over at the altar. "That for me?"

Micah took a breath and said, "Yes, if you like it. Sir."

"Ah, don't 'sir' me," the man, no, the spirit, said, and moved to the altar. "You can call me...Terran."

Micah watched as Terran stepped lightly over to the altar and looked down at the offerings. He picked up the chicken eggs one by one and turned them in his hands. Each disappeared to a place that Micah could not see. He picked up the bottle of milk and tore off the thin paper covering, drinking the whole thing in a few greedy swallows. The rolls he examined, squirreling one away for later, then taking a few bites of the other. He picked up the ribbon and cocked his head to the side.

"What's this?" he asked, turning to Micah.

"A ribbon," Micah said, feeling extremely foolish.

Terran snorted, and said, "Yeah, can see that. Why are you offering it to me?"

"The guardian spirit in the forest by my old home sometimes liked pretty things," Micah said, trying to meet those green eyes and failing. "I thought you might like it? I'm sorry if I caused any offense."

Terran stood, quickly for his size, and said, "No offense. 'Tis pretty, no doubt."

"If you don't like it, I can just stick to food next time. If that's better," Micah said, gripping the strap of his satchel like a vise to keep his hands from shaking. This was the first time he had ever properly spoken to anything otherworldly.

Terran grinned and tilted his head again, saying, "Nah, I like pretty things."

Micah's mouth went dry, but he just nodded. Terran was lacing the yellow ribbon between his fingers and chewing on the bread. Micah didn't know if he was allowed to leave, and he didn't want to cause offense, especially on his first visit to these woods. But he couldn't help shuffling his feet slightly.

"Been a long time since I had a proper offering," Terran said, finishing the bread roll.

"Oh?" Micah said, genuinely surprised. He had thought that Roseyard had a lumber business.

"Yeah," Terran said, moving closer to Micah again. "Appreciate it. Most of the townsfolk just take with no regard."

"I am sorry," Micah said, shock rolling through him. "I won't take too much, I promise."

Terran smiled a lopsided grin and said, "You take as much as you like, sweet thing. You at least know how to respect the forest."

Micah blanched at the pet name but nodded and said, "Thank you. I can't take too much credit. My mother taught me."

"Taught you well, it seems," Terran said, closing the distance between them. "What are we after? I'll see what I can do."

"Oh!" Micah said, shocked again. "You're coming with me? Sorry, that was rude, of course you're welcome to. It's your forest, after all."

Terran clapped a large hand on Micah's shoulder and laughed, a deep, rich sound that echoed and played through the trees, then said, "Relax! You're doing fine. Nicest human I've ever spoken to, that's for damn sure."

Micah's face got hot and he said, "Thank you, sir. Terran. I'm just looking for honey, that's the thing I truly need. If I find anything else, that would be wonderful, but I do need the honey."

"Mmm," Terran said thoughtfully. "Can help you with that, for sure."

Micah smiled and said, "Oh, thank you, so much. Truly."

Terran grinned at him, and Micah thought for a moment that he saw an inchworm crawling through the strands of his beard. A robin darted down from a tree and landed on Terran's shoulder, chirping away. Terran listened for a moment, then whistled back at the bird in an impossible melody. This seemed to satisfy the robin and it flew away.

"Funny little thing," Terran said, releasing another rumbling laugh.

Then he grabbed Micah's hand with a strong but gentle grip and pulled him through the trees. Micah thought he would stumble, since Terran's legs were much longer and he made his way through the forest with deft, magical precision. But no, with Terran's steady hand on his, Micah traveled with that same ease. It was strange to step in mud and not be bogged down.

"New here, then?" Terran asked suddenly. "What brought you to the town?"

"Ah, well," Micah said, swallowing down some unpleasant memories and rubbing at the scars on his throat. "Had some trouble where I used to live, came out here for a fresh start."

"Not bringing me trouble, I hope?" Terran asked, turning to him with that lopsided smile.

"No, I won't," Micah said sincerely, a pang shooting through his heart. "That should all be left behind."

"Just teasing," Terran said with a shrug. "Apologies. What do you do?"

"My mother and I used to keep bees, then bake and make soap, medicine, whatnot. She was a witch, I just helped her." Micah wet his lips and swallowed. "But, well, the trouble. I don't have the hives anymore."

"Huh," Terran said, stopping suddenly and turning to look at Micah.

He took Micah's chin in one large hand, holding his head in place. Micah couldn't do anything but stare back up at him. Terran seemed to be counting each freckle on his face and searching his brown eyes. His eyes dropped to the scars on Micah's throat, a frown playing on his lips. He seemed to make an assessment and dropped Micah's chin, then kept walking, taking Micah along with him.

"Sorry for what happened to you," Terran said.

"I…" Micah fell silent for a moment before continuing, "Did you read my mind or something?"

Micah's heart raced, his face and the tips of his ears burned, and he wanted nothing more than to tear his eyes away from those deep, green ones. He hoped that Terran hadn't seen into his thoughts. There was so much in him that he didn't want anyone to see, didn't want anyone to know, much less a spirit of the forest. Terran didn't need to know what Micah had buried deep, deep underground. No one needed to know that.

"No, can't do that," Terran said. "But I can tell you're hurting."

Micah was quiet again, and Terran was as well. They moved under the trees with that same ease, but there was something different about Terran that Micah couldn't quite put his finger on. Soon, though, he heard a familiar buzzing that brought a smile to his face. The hive was up in the tree branches, but that had never stopped him. It looked to be rather large and healthy. Wonderful. He'd be able to take a decent amount.

"Thank you, sir," Micah said, then winced and corrected himself again. "Terran. This is perfect."

Terran smiled at Micah and let go of his hand. He leaned back against a nearby tree and watched Micah with careful eyes. Micah assessed the tree and found his footholds. He adjusted his hat and up he went. Most people were surprised how good Micah was at climbing, but he grew up in the forest, climbing trees for his mother and her bad knee. It was second nature to him.

He reached the hive and carefully, with a beekeeper's precision, started taking what he needed. He hung the basket, with a handkerchief lining the bottom, on a nearby branch. He reached into his bag and retrieved a hunting knife. A particularly kind gentleman named Barton had gifted it to him on his journey to Roseyard after Micah had helped his sick daughter's sore throat. It had taken the last of his honey from his old home. The man had thanked Micah and called him a hedgewitch in front of his daughter, despite Micah's insistence that he was not a witch. He had no magic to speak of.

He used the lovely knife to delicately pull off pieces of honeycomb, careful not to take any pieces with babies inside, and very careful to avoid the queen. There was just one bee who stung him; the rest were unbothered. He hadn't lost his touch after all. After a few minutes, he carefully descended with about two dozen healthy pieces of comb.

As he landed on the ground, he dipped a finger into the honey, then rubbed it on the sting to stop the pain. Terran was watching him with a rather impressed look on his face. Micah smiled and broke off a piece of comb, offering it to him. Terran grinned and took it, popping it into his mouth with satisfaction. Micah broke off a slightly smaller piece for himself and chewed it, savoring the sweet, wild taste. It had been far too long since he had proper wild honey.

"Thank you," Micah said, smiling.

"What else do you need?" Terran said, cocking his head to the side, a habit of his that made him seem far more like a wild beast than anything more closely related to Micah.

"I was just going to look for any herbs, maybe mushrooms or berries," Micah said. "But nothing pressing."

"What you gave was worth more than a few combs of honey, come along."

Micah found himself once again being led through the forest, but they were moving more quickly now. The trees streamed past them at an impossible speed. Terran would stop once in a while to point something out, a litter of fox kits or a stag in the forest, grinning when Micah listened and watched carefully. He brought Micah to a bush full of berries and encouraged him to take as many as he wanted. He gathered a bounty of oyster mushrooms and chicken of the woods, weighing down Micah's basket. Plants, some like mint and wild garlic, others like wood sorrel and yarrow, soon filled Micah's bag.

"Terran, I can't thank you enough," Micah said as Terran dumped blackberries into his basket. "I don't think I could take anything else."

"Right," Terran said, those wild green eyes looking at the basket and bag. "Better get you home."

"Could you take me back to where you found me in the forest?" Micah said. "I have a little cottage not far from the tree line."

"Going to come visit again?" Terran asked, that lopsided smile on his face.

"Of course," Micah said, then after a pause, "If you don't mind, that is. I'll of course bring offerings. Did that altar work for you?"

Terran grinned and tilted his head. "More than all right with me, my sweet. Glad to see you again."

Micah smiled back, only pausing for a small moment at Terran calling him 'sweet' again, and said, "I would of course be honored if you graced me with your presence again, Terran."

"So fancy," Terran said, that deep, resounding laugh echoing off the trees. "No need for all that."

"Oh, all right," Micah said, reddening again. "I'm sorry."

"You're turning as red as a blister, why?"

"I-I don't know, sorry."

"You don't need to apologize."

Micah stood, weighed down by gifts from the forest, and stared at the guardian spirit, who had taken the shape of a gentle, strong man and was looking at him with deep kindness. That look was so tender that Micah almost wanted to cry, but instead he just smiled and nodded. Terran took his arm and soon they were back at the makeshift altar. Micah grabbed the bottle to return to his neighbor, bowed deeply to Terran, thanking him once again, then moved to leave.

Terran was there beside him faster than Micah's eyes could track. He wordlessly looped his arm through Micah's and he walked with him to the edge of the forest. The trees grew further and further apart, rolling out into a clear grassy field. It wasn't too far across that field to the small cottage where he lived. When they got to the last tree, Micah gently pulled his arm back and smiled at Terran.

"Thank you once again," he said, then, feeling a bit bold, asked, "Would you like tea? I know you can't leave the forest, but I could go back to the house, make it, and bring it to you here. If you like."

Terran tilted his head with a sad smile, then said, "I would love some, but not today. Duties to attend to. But maybe next time."

"All right," Micah said. "And thank you."

Terran placed a finger on Micah's mouth, silencing him. "You have thanked me many times."

Micah didn't say anything, shocked into silence at the warmth of the finger against his lips. Then Terran took his hand and lifted it. He unlaced the yellow ribbon from between his fingers, then tied it around Micah's wrist in a bow. Terran ran his fingers against the sensitive skin on Micah's inner wrist, making gooseflesh break out down his arms. Micah looked up at him and smiled, then Terran's mouth grew into a grin as warm as the noontime sun.

"Do come back," he said. "I like pretty things."

"Oh," was all Micah could manage before he blinked and Terran was gone.

2

THE MARKET

Micah had five days until the market and so much to do. The ginger cookies would wait until the day before, but he could get started on his other products. The reasonable voice within him, the voice that sounded much like his mother, told him to focus on a few things instead of everything. It would be his first market in Roseyard, and he was running low on silver. He decided to stick with the three big sellers that had always done well: soap, candles, and ginger cookies. If he had enough honey left over, he'd make honey drops as well.

After his strange and marvelous foraging trip, he checked on his five hens in their little hutch. They were all happily in the yard, pecking at the ground. He watched them for a moment, smiling and leaning on the fence as the big, fat brown hen looked up at him. He had gotten them from a woman as he came south to Roseyard. Lillian, her name was, and she and her brothers were taking quite a few animals down to sell. She offered Micah five hens for five silver and some clothes of his mother's. He felt sad parting with them, but he truly could not beat the price. And now he also had eggs to eat or trade or offer…He ran his finger across the smooth yellow ribbon tied around his wrist.

He moved on from the hens to the herb garden where Wilbur, his donkey, was dutifully eating from his portion of the patch. Really, the herbs were still growing in at this point, but he watered them, weeded a bit, and then stroked Wilbur's neck quietly. Wilbur was old, older than Micah was by a couple of years. Micah buried his face against Wilbur, wrapping his arms around his dear old friend.

"I met someone today, Wilbur," Micah said quietly against the donkey's neck. "Someone incredible. It was a guardian spirit, can you believe it?"

Wilbur snorted softly and lifted his head to snuffle against Micah's neck. Micah smiled and promised a carrot for him later and moved inside the cottage. He started sorting through the basket with all of the gifts, a bit overwhelmed at the rather large bounty. His stores simply hadn't been prepared for all this. He set aside the glass bottle to bring back to Marion and collected some of the berries and mushrooms to give to her in exchange for her wood ash.

After stopping to give Wilbur the promised carrot and scatter some more grain for the hens, he began the twenty-minute-long trek to Marion's house. Marion Beath was a cranky old woman who had lived alone since her husband passed twenty years earlier, and she was determined to outlive everyone who was ever rude to her. It was an impossible task, but if anyone could do it, it would be Marion. She kept dairy cows, and Micah had convinced her to trade a bottle of milk for six eggs from his hens the day before.

Her cottage was entirely practical. Not one small piece of decoration graced its exterior, and not a single thing was askew. Micah dusted himself off and took a deep breath before he knocked on the door. From within, he heard a chair pushed back from the table and stomping feet accompanied by shouts of "I told you for the last time Mr. Fenwick, my house is not for…."

The door flew open and the rage on Marion's wrinkled face dissipated as she saw Micah standing there. "Oh! Mr. Harlow. Thought you were someone else. Come in, come in."

Micah followed her into the house, as practical inside as it was out with the small concession of a couple of tiny wood carvings of cows sitting on the mantel. Apparently Marion had been making cheese when he had come knocking. Micah's mouth started to water; it had been a very long time since he had been able to afford cheese.

"Caught me at a busy time," Marion said, clearing a seat at the table for Micah and his basket. "This won't be ready for this market, of course, but you've got to plan."

"Of course," Micah said, smiling at her. "I brought back your bottle, thank you very much."

He offered it to her and she plucked it from his hands as she said, "You didn't make that last very long, now did you?"

"Ah, well, it wasn't for me," Micah said. "But I do have another trade offer for you. I gathered some berries and mushrooms in the woods this morning. They're quite good. I was wondering if you'd be willing to trade your wood ash for them?"

Marion stared at him as he produced a small basket full of berries and then unwrapped some of the best of the oyster mushrooms. He wasn't quite desperate enough to give up his chicken of the woods yet. The look she gave him made his smile falter slightly.

"Or maybe something else?" he said tentatively.

"You went into the woods?" Marion asked, eyebrows knitting together as she looked him up and down. "Did no one warn you? Well, of course not, you're new here, you wouldn't know. And you've only spoken with me as far as I know, and I thought you wouldn't be fool enough to go in there. My mistake, it seems."

"I was only foraging," Micah said, a bit surprised at the reaction. "I used to do it in the woods near Steephall all the time."

"But there wasn't a *beast* in Steephall's forest, I'd wager," Marion said.

"A beast?" Micah repeated, blessing his good luck that he had only run into Terran.

"Looks like a man, they say, with eyes as wild and green as the forest itself, the antlers of a stag sticking out from his head," Marion said, leaning in conspiratorially. "He'll snatch up young people and lead them away, gobble them up in his forest hold."

"Oh!" Micah said, unable to keep the note of surprise out of his voice. "Oh, no. I believe that's the guardian spirit that you are referring to. He means only to protect the forest, and is quite helpful if you leave him an offering. That's who the milk was for."

"You met the beast?" Marion said, her eyes widening to an unnatural width and her mouth falling open. "You gave him milk? My milk?"

"Not really a beast," Micah said with a light-hearted huff of laughter. "But a powerful spirit. He was rather grateful for the offering. Every forest has a guardian, you know."

Marion was silent for a long moment, then said, "You best not tell anyone in the village you met it. And you best not go in that forest again."

"He's a guardian spirit," Micah said.

"I don't think our forest has a guardian, Mr. Harlow," Marion said. "Only ones bold enough to go in there on their own would be warlocks. You're not a warlock, are you?"

She eyed him suspiciously, her bright eyes roving up and down his frame. Micah swallowed and tried not to let that accusation sting as much as it did. He gripped the rim of the basket to keep from reaching up and touching the scars on his throat. Instead, he painted what he hoped looked like an easy smile on his face.

"Not a warlock, no, but my mother was a hedgewitch," Micah said. "I helped her a lot when I was younger. I've dealt with guardian spirits before. As long as you leave them an offering, you're safe."

But in his memory, the look of curiosity in Terran's eyes shifted into something much hungrier. A familiar, predatory hunger. He shook his head to dislodge the false image. Marion was looking now at the berries with an entirely different kind of hunger.

"Well, Mr. Harlow," Marion said. "As long as you are being safe. Your mother was a hedgewitch? Are you one as well? I've got this terrible ache in my lower back, if you could take a look?"

"Ah, no, sadly I never picked up the knack. No casting spells for me," Micah said, shrugging with an actually easy smile. "I don't have her recipe book anymore, otherwise I'd brew you up something. That much I could do. But I'll be sure to think it over, and I'll let you know if I remember anything."

"A shame," Marion said with a sigh. "It's been a long time since Roseyard has had a proper hedgewitch. That would have been handy."

Micah bit back a comment about how it seemed that Roseyard had lost the old ways if they weren't sacrificing to the spirit and it was no wonder that there wasn't a hedgewitch here. Witches respected the spirits of the world, and while he wasn't one himself, he understood why they would steer clear of a place that so clearly didn't.

"Well, maybe I can try a few of the tricks my mother taught me," Micah said, trying to sound cheerful. "Bring back a bit of witchery. At least I'm not a warlock, right?"

Micah laughed, but Marion didn't. She just eyed him suspiciously again, and all he could do was hope that it hadn't been a misstep. She tapped her fingers on the table.

"Not quite something to joke about," Marion said, staring into his eyes. "Warlocks are dangerous. They're selfish, greedy. Are you sure that the creature you encountered was a guardian spirit, as you say, and not the beast? Not a demon?"

"I'm sure. I am familiar with this, I promise," Micah said, then changed the subject as quickly as he could. "Could I have your wood ash? In exchange for the bounty. If you don't mind."

"You are welcome to my wood ash, boy. I'll take your berries and mushrooms, but not as payment for that. I'll stay quiet about you going into the woods."

"Is that really such a crime?" Micah said, once again surprised that Roseyard seemed to have so badly lost its way.

"It simply isn't done," Marion said. "Have a good day, Mr. Harlow."

Micah knew a dismissal when he heard one, so he tipped his hat and got up from the table, leaving the berries and mushrooms behind. He quickly found the wood ash and scooped it into the box that he had brought along, the conversation playing back in his mind again and again.

The rest of the day he spent making lye, pouring hot water carefully over the wicker sieve that held the ashes. Occasionally, he'd eat a berry, popping it into his mouth and savoring the flavor, thinking back to Terran and his wild green eyes.

The next days were full of his work, mixing the lye with birch oil, then shaping it into the soap cakes, embedding them with lavender or rosemary, thyme or a few drops of honey. Soon his little cottage smelled heavenly.

He scraped every ounce of honey from the combs into waiting jars. He hummed the song his mother had always sung while she did this, the strange words long since lost to him but the melody with him forever. She had explained the meaning to him once when he was young. She said it was a wish, a hope for health and happiness for all who ate the honey. Warmth bloomed in his chest at the thought, and he hummed louder as he worked. He set out the comb to rest, then spun the honey or strained it through cloth, depending on its purpose.

The combs he then set to softening over the fire until the wax was pliable and could be formed into fat little candles. They weren't bad for his first attempt in nearly a year, and he smiled proudly at them lined up on his table like little soldiers waiting to march to war.

While doing this, he continued to care for his garden, his chickens, his donkey. As he worked outside, his eyes always drifted to the tree line. More than once he would have sworn he felt eyes upon him, watching as he pulled weeds or gathered eggs. He imagined eyes as verdant and deep as the forest itself dancing across him. He made sure that the yellow ribbon stayed tied around his wrist, tightening it each time it threatened to abandon him.

THE DAY BEFORE THE MARKET WAS BAKING DAY. HE ROSE EARLY and tended to the hens and Wilbur, then dedicated the rest of the day to working over the oven. Flour, cinnamon, ginger, and honey: his hands were soon embedded with the scents of the ingredients. He hummed to himself the songs that his mother had sung while they made these cookies long ago as he shaped them into balls, then placed them in the hot oven.

Mix and knead the dough, hum the song about shaping your future and holding your dreams in your heart. Roll it into little balls, hum the song about making a home and filling it with love. Put them in the oven, hum the song about safety and warmth, joy and laughter. Over and over, until the air was filled with music as well as the smell of the cookies. He always felt so at peace when he did this, each song filling his chest and his soul as he hummed it. It had been too long.

A cloud of nostalgia and sweetness filled the cottage as the cookies baked to perfection. Micah leaned against the wall letting the smell wash over him and thinking of the hundreds of times he had made these with his mother. They had made them with love back then, and he did the same now. He hummed the songs again, just for himself, just to feel that glow of memory as the melody resonated in his head and the scent of the cookies filled him.

Baskets started filling with cookies as his supply of flour ran lower and lower throughout the day. He would need to visit the miller and get more while he was in town the next day. He still had plenty of honey—he had been able to gather much more than he had anticipated—and he started making honey drops while the last batch of cookies was in the oven.

Water and sugar, a bit of the expensive lemon juice, and of course honey. It boiled over his fire and he pulled out the small, sticky balls to cool on the dark stone slab. They were delicious, yes, but they were also wonderful on a sore throat. He powdered them with sugar and placed them in about five different glass jars. The cottage was full of the sweet scent and the music of Micah's humming. It was near evening when he was finally done, and he still needed to load up Wilbur's cart for the next day.

However, he set aside two very important sets of the cookies, candies, and soaps. One was for Marion; he would also take some eggs to her in exchange for milk, and maybe some cheese. The other was for Terran. Despite Marion's warning, Micah would have to go back into the forest, if only for the honey. At least until he could afford his own hives, but still. The forest was not as dangerous as Marion seemed to think. He ran a finger across the yellow ribbon and smiled.

Marion, it turned out, was thrilled to receive the cookies and other gifts, along with six eggs, and gave him two bottles of milk and a healthy hunk of cheese. Micah returned to his cottage and cut off about half the cheese for himself, but placed the other half and the two bottles of milk with his gifts for Terran.

Before the sun set, he loaded up the small cart with his baskets of soap cakes, candles, cookies, and candy. He draped a tarp over it to protect the contents from any sudden, unpredictable rainstorms and gave Wilbur a carrot for his trouble. The donkey would stand guard over the cart as diligently as he had always stood guard over Micah. As the golden rays turned to orange and rust and dipped behind the trees of the wood, Micah could swear that he saw a tall man standing there, leaning lazily against a tree and watching him.

MICAH ROSE BEFORE THE SUN, TOOK CARE OF THE HENS, leaving them roosted since Wilbur wouldn't be there to watch over them, and hitched up his donkey to head into town. The hazy early morning light mixed with a mist that rolled from the forest across the fields, giving the world a dreamlike veneer. Micah found himself humming again, a soft song that his mother used to sing to him long ago. This one, he thought he could have remembered the words if he really tried. She had sung it so often. It was about safety in traveling, protection, and luck. It had been the perfect market day song, and Micah continued the tradition.

He had conferred with the townhead a week before and secured a location where his small board would be set up. Of course, it wasn't the ideal position, but that was to be expected until they knew him better. There were already several booths set up in the town square. Many of them were far more elaborate and eye-catching than his would be, but that was just fine. He hitched Wilbur with a group of other donkeys and then pulled the cart the rest of the way to his designated spot himself.

He first set up the boards and then started laying out the candles and soap cakes. He was arranging the jars of honey candy when the holder of the board next to his arrived. She was an extremely tired-looking young woman with dull reddish hair that fell in tangles around her face and deep purple bruising under her gray eyes. He smiled and tipped his straw hat to her, which only got a small nod and an odd look in response.

"You're new," she said flatly.

"Good morning! I'm Micah Harlow. I moved in out by Mrs. Marion Beath's place 'bout a month ago," Micah said, cheerfully but not loudly in case a hangover was to blame for the young woman's appearance. "First time at the market though."

"Huh," she said. "All right. I'm Kay."

Micah held out a hand to shake hers. She snorted, a brief look of amusement sweeping across her face, but she took the offered hand. She set up her own board, spreading out an intricately stitched cloth but nothing else. The final touch was a small, ancient-looking stool that she set on the ground, then sat on without ceremony.

Micah was letting his eyes drift over to her in curiosity as he set out the first basket of cookies and she suddenly perked up. She stood and looked over at the cookies, sniffing the air, then licked her lips.

"How much for one of those?" she asked, digging into her skirts for money.

"Ah!" Micah grinned. "For my neighbor, the first one is free!"

"That's bad business, how much?" she said, her voice staying flat and tired.

"Oh, but—" Micah started to say, but was cut off.

"I won't take charity. How much?" she repeated.

"A bit for one, or three for two bits," Micah said, holding up his hands.

"Great," she said, and tossed him a bit, snatching a cookie from the basket. "Better not hear a higher price from you when the customers come around."

"I wouldn't dare," Micah said with a smile. "But it wasn't charity, just friendliness. I promise."

Kay had taken a bite of the cookie and was chewing thoughtfully. The pupils of her eyes dilated slightly and she put a hand to her lips. She gave a sudden surprised *mmm* and ate the rest greedily.

"That is good," she said, looking over at him in surprise. "Really good. I should have gotten three for two."

"Give me another bit and I'll give you two more," Micah said. "As an act of friendliness."

Kay seemed to weigh the thought against her apparent repulsion against charity, then nodded. She pressed the second bit into his hand this time and grabbed two of the cookies, placing them on the embroidered cloth on her board.

"What is it that you sell, Kay?" Micah asked.

"Oh, you don't know?" Kay said, her brows furrowing.

"New in town," Micah said, smiling at her again.

"Huh, but no one told you?" she asked. "The townhead didn't tell you that you've got the cursed booth?"

"Cursed?" Micah asked, hoping that his fear and concern didn't bleed through into his voice.

He had sometimes thought he was cursed—the bad luck after his mother's death that followed him around like a miasma seemed evidence of that—but in reality he doubted it. Warlocks laid curses, and he had never met a warlock in his life. That he knew of. Though it could have been a spirit, or a demon, but he couldn't imagine what he could have done to draw their ire.

"Well, by association. I'm a sin-eater," Kay said, snapping him out of his thoughts. There was hesitation in her voice.

"Oh!" Micah said. "Oh, wow! I've never met a sin-eater before. It's an honor."

Kay scrutinized him for sarcasm or humor in his voice, but she continued carefully, "You're strange."

"Maybe," Micah said, smiling again. "But, sorry if I'm ignorant about this, don't people only need your services with the dead? Are there that many dead folks here in Roseyard?"

Kay looked him up and down with tired eyes before she tucked a tangled piece of hair behind her ear and said, "I eat the sins of the living too. It's…a family talent."

Micah waited for her to continue, but she seemed finished. She picked up another cookie and continued to nibble at it. He had never heard of a sin-eater who could eat the sins of the living before, but his mother had always told him that magic was far more wild and unique than the small categories that the world had made for people touched by it. There were magical talents that were limited to just small families. This must be one of them, and Micah itched to ask more, but he didn't dare push his neighbor more today.

Micah finished setting up his booth and sat waiting for customers. As the sun moved up in the sky, they arrived. The smell of the cookies worked wonders. He had plenty of business, more than he was expecting if he were completely honest. People would drift over for the cookies, then buy soap or candles, walking away already smelling better than before. The honey candies were less of a hit, but he still sold plenty of them. He was constantly busy, exchanging goods for coins and speaking with each person in his practiced friendly manner. The citizens of Roseyard were very curious about their newest neighbor, even if he technically lived outside of town.

Occasionally, out of the corner of his eye, he'd spot someone at Kay's booth. They would exchange a few soft words, then an absurd amount of coin, and Kay would reach out to the patron's chest and pluck out a wriggling black snake of smoke. She would then open her mouth and slurp it down, a sour look on her face.

At a quiet moment between customers for both of them, after she had eaten a particularly large and foul looking sin, Micah popped off the lid of a jar of honey candy and held it out to her. She looked at the candies, seeming to debate telling him to shove them somewhere unpleasant before she sighed and took one, placing it on her tongue and sucking on it.

"How much?" she asked around the candy.

"It's a bit for three," Micah said. "But I'll let you have as many as you like while we're neighbors if I can use your services later."

Kay propped her head on her hand, glanced over at him, and nodded. After that, she would occasionally hold out her hand after one of her clients and Micah would drop a honey candy into her palm. He sometimes caught her staring at him, surely trying to figure out what sin of his he wanted her to eat.

As noon rolled around, an extremely well-dressed man started strolling down the aisles of the market, stopping occasionally to speak with a vendor or to the townsfolk. He wore a well-cut suit made of thick wool. His slick black hair was pulled back into a tail, tied snugly with a silk ribbon the same shade of blue as the suit. His shoes actually gleamed in the sunlight. He was an extremely large man, much like Terran was, but where Terran's body was that of a steady old tree, this man moved like a predatory cat. His was a cruel body, seemingly poised to inflict harm on whatever displeased him. When she spotted him, Kay sat up straight on her little stool and folded her hands in front of her, eyes dipped down.

The man approached her table with what Micah could only describe as a wicked grin and looked down at her as he twisted a large brass ring on his finger. "Hello, Miss Lindon. Do you have your payment ready for this month?"

"Yes, sir," she said, reaching into her skirts to pull out a purse.

Despite his finery, the man had little respect for decorum. He dumped the contents of the purse onto the table with a clash of metal coins. Kay winced. The customer at Micah's booth paid quickly and scurried away, tucking into the cookies as they left. The man counted the coins, nodded, then scooped them back into the purse.

"You are far better at this than your brother, Miss Lindon," the man said. "Thank you for your payment."

"Of course, Mr. Fenwick," Kay said.

Kay had seemed tired before, but now she actually seemed scared. Her hands were shaking, quivering against the cloth, and she stared down at them, refusing to look up into the cruel face above her. Then, as if she were nothing more than an annoying gnat, he brushed away from her and started to stride down the street, but then he sniffed the air. He turned back to Micah's booth.

"Hmm," he said, looking at Micah. "I don't think I recognize you."

"Oh," Micah said, painting on a smile. "Micah Harlow. I recently moved to Roseyard."

He tipped his straw hat and offered a hand. Mr. Fenwick looked down at it in momentary confusion before taking it and pumping it once in the way that men who wanted to make their strength known always did. He smiled a wolfish grin with not a smidge of humor or kindness.

"Charles Fenwick," he said. "A pleasure to meet you, Mr. Harlow.

Pray tell, where did you move? I don't remember anyone coming into town and I make a point of knowing everyone here."

"Oh, the little cottage out by Marion Beath's place," Micah said, keeping his voice light and easy. "She sold it to me since it wasn't being used."

"Quite," Fenwick said, his eyes narrowing. "Well, it must be fate that we met here today, then, Mr. Harlow. I've been trying to buy up that land for quite some time now. I would love to make an offer to you."

"Ah, well," Micah said, tilting his head to the side. "Just got settled in there is the thing. I don't think I plan on selling it anytime soon."

"I can make it worth your trouble," Fenwick said, that wolfish grin coming back. "I'll pay you far more than that land is worth."

"I'll think on it," Micah said, if only to appease that grin. "But I wouldn't get your hopes up. I'm sorry."

"Well, if you change your mind," he said, spreading out his hands, "ask for me in town and I'll be found easily enough. That I can promise. Now, what are these that smell so delicious?"

Charles Fenwick bought a dozen cookies, an entire jar of the honey candy, five soap cakes, and a bundle of candles. Micah saw precisely what he was doing, showing just how wealthy he was and attempting to get onto Micah's good side by showering him with money.

"You're braver than most," Kay muttered to him once Fenwick had left.

"How so?" Micah asked, glancing over at her and giving her another honey drop.

"Most won't say no to Charles Fenwick," Kay said. "Though you did say it in a clever way, so good on you for that."

"Who is Charles Fenwick?"

"He owns half the town, my family is up to our eyeballs in debt and we're far from the only ones," Kay said softly. "How can you say no to someone who can rip your life away?"

Another couple of customers came up, which stopped the conversation in its tracks, but Micah knew what Kay meant. There were men everywhere who thought that because they had money and power, the world was theirs to play with. Fenwick seemed exactly the kind to believe that. Thinking of the last time he had met a man like that, Micah rubbed the scars at his throat.

The rest of the market went smoothly; Micah made far more money than he had expected and was quite pleased. He glanced over and was surprised to see that Kay's purse appeared to be even lighter than it had been at the start of the market. That had been the work of Charles Fenwick. Her face was twisted up in a scowl as she weighed the pouch in her hand, but soon she sighed heavily and started packing up.

As Micah loaded up the leftover goods and his boards into the cart, Kay came up to him, took him by the shoulders, and turned him around. She was just a bit taller than him, and she looked down at him with watery gray eyes.

"Time for me to pay for those candies," she said.

"Oh, this wasn't what I meant when I said later," he said with a smile. "I don't have anything that I need taken from me right now. Sometime, in the future, sure! But for now, my candy jar remains open to you."

Kay's face twisted in disbelief and then she said, defeated, "You tricked me."

"Not tricked," Micah said, then thought, and added, "All right, maybe tricked. But out of friendliness, *not* charity."

"Kindness, more like it," Kay said.

"Kindness comes around threefold," Micah said, bouncing a bit on his toes. "And it's just, nice to be nice."

After a moment, she sighed as though he were the most naive person in all the world, but said, "Thank you. And thank you for not judging."

"Never would," Micah said with a smile.

They parted ways with a friendly wave from Micah and a tired one from Kay. Micah had a few more tasks before he could head home. He bought more flour, first, and he would definitely need it. Only crumbs were left of the ginger cookies. He bought dried meat, some more vegetables as well as seeds to grow his own, and some flowers just because they made him smile.

As he was moving through the market, he spotted an old woman selling jewelry. There was a necklace hanging from the corner of the canopy over her table, the silver catching the sunlight and sparkling. Micah turned the pendant to face him. Carved in its face was a five-petaled flower. With the words *I like pretty things* echoing in his mind, he bought it. He tucked it into his trouser pocket and once again ran his fingers across the yellow ribbon around his wrist.

3

THE OFFERING

The day after the market, Micah made his way into the woods laden with gifts for Terran. He hummed happily as he followed the path to the altar he had set up. It was an old song of his mother's, of course, a song about happiness and contentment. It must have been his imagination, but the sun through the branches felt warmer, the birds sang sweeter, and his steps were lighter.

Micah found the altar and immediately began cleaning it up. He brushed off the dirt, rearranged stones that had fallen, and started setting out the offerings. Two bottles of milk this time, six ginger cookies, ten honey drops, a large piece of cheese, a lavender soap cake, another three eggs and two bread rolls, and finally the necklace he had bought at the market.

Micah arranged all the items and then pulled out a candle laced with sage. He was about to strike the flint when a hand landed on top of his.

"Save your candle, my sweet, I heard you coming as soon as you stumbled past the tree line," Terran rumbled in his ear.

Micah spun around on his knees, which made him topple and land on his back, looking up at a very amused Terran. His hat had gone flying, but better that than it being crushed beneath him. Terran sat on the ground, crossing his legs and tilting his head to the side as he watched Micah pick himself up.

"Apologies," he said. "I didn't mean to scare you."

"It's quite all right, Terran," Micah said, brushing dirt off of himself, quite grateful that it hadn't rained that week and he wasn't rolling in mud. "I just didn't expect it and, well, it seems I'm rather clumsy."

Terran smiled, looking Micah over carefully as he sat down across from him, then leaned forward to tuck a curl behind his ear. Once again, Micah found himself frozen as Terran touched him. Terran's eyes drifted down to Micah's wrist where the yellow ribbon was still tied. He looked back up at Micah with that lopsided grin.

"Well, let's see what you brought me," Terran said, turning to the altar.

Terran crawled over to it in an animalistic way that Micah wasn't quite expecting. He picked up each item carefully and examined it, squirreling away the eggs and bread again and drinking the milk. He looked at the cookies and candies with curiosity.

"Sweets?" he asked, turning back to look at Micah.

"You helped me to gather the honey I used to make them, so I supposed that maybe I should share them with you," Micah said, feeling a blush creeping up his neck.

"Which is best?" Terran asked, holding up a cookie and a honey drop.

"I like the cookies better, personally," Micah said, gesturing.

"Hmm," Terran said before taking a large bite.

His eyes widened, pupils dilating and hand going to his lips in a strange mirror of Kay from the day before. His nostrils flared and he looked at Micah as he ate the rest of the cookie in another large bite, chewing it and savoring it. Then he was suddenly in front of Micah, grabbing his wrists, his face mere inches from Micah's.

"You made this?" he asked, eyes still wide.

"Yes, I did," Micah squeaked out in surprise.

Realizing what he was doing, Terran dropped Micah's wrists and sat back before saying, "Very good."

"Oh, thank you," Micah said. "I used to make them with my mother."

"Used to? What, did she lose the trick of it?" Terran asked, sitting back at the altar and picking up another cookie.

"She died," Micah said softly.

Terran looked up at him in surprise, then shook his head and said, "Apologies. I didn't mean to make light."

Micah shrugged and said, "You didn't know. It's all right."

"The magic in them was lovely," Terran said. "Very sweet, very kind."

"There wasn't any magic in them," Micah said, blinking with surprise. "I mean, my mother was a witch, but I'm not."

"Are you sure?" Terran asked, tilting his head. "I thought I tasted magic."

Micah didn't say anything, just shook his head. Terran squirreled away the cookies and candies wherever the eggs had disappeared to, then picked up the soap. He ran his fingers across the cake and lifted it to his nose, inhaling deeply. He made a couple of humming noises before turning back to Micah.

"Soap? Are you saying I am dirty?" he asked, a lopsided grin on his face.

"Oh! No! No, not at all what I meant!" Micah lifted his hands in alarm and said, "I am so sorry, I didn't mean to insinuate…I just make soap and I thought that it could be a good gift, but I promise I wasn't—"

Terran cut him off with his big booming laugh, following it with, "I'm not cross. Don't worry. You worry too much, I think."

Micah let out a nervous laugh, but his heart was beating hard. He needed to think more carefully about his offerings if he was going to be in this forest often. Terran, however, seemed to take it all in stride. He picked up the cheese and took a bite, then, glancing back at Micah, smiled and broke off a piece, offering it to him.

"Oh, no," Micah said, shaking his head. "That's for you."

"And I would like to share it," Terran said, grinning at him. "I can tell that you want some."

Micah, embarrassed, took the offered piece and nibbled on it. He had really wanted it, but he felt guilty taking an offering back from the recipient.

Finally, he watched as Terran picked up the last thing on the altar. The silver necklace. He let it turn in the sun, holding it up and letting it sparkle in his eyes.

"I remember you said that you liked pretty things," Micah said.

Terran turned back to him and grinned. "Pretty flower on it. It'll remind me of you. Flowers in the hat and all."

Micah smiled nervously and nodded. He watched as Terran unhooked the clasp and moved to put it on. He was struggling to catch the clasp again behind his head, and Micah moved carefully closer, then set his hands softly on Terran's fingers.

"Here, let me," Micah said.

He gently took the chain and easily caught the clasp. He let go and let the necklace slide into place as he swallowed. Terran turned around and smiled at him. Micah smiled back and then jumped as Terran popped Micah's hat back on his head.

"Thank you kindly," Terran said as he stood up with incredible ease. "Now, what do you need today? Same as last time?"

"Yes," Micah said, still reeling a bit.

"Great!" Terran said, then reached down and tugged Micah to his feet.

Once again, they spent a day moving through the trees gathering things for Micah. Micah kept insisting that it was too much, but Terran wouldn't hear of it. He ended up carrying the basket when it grew too heavy for Micah and filled the air with chatter about the forest.

"What's it like?" Micah asked as they broke for a small rest by a stream, more for Micah than Terran, obviously.

"What's *what* like?" Terran asked, cocking his head.

"Being the guardian of the forest?" Micah asked, cupping water from the stream and bringing it to his mouth.

Terran considered the question for a long time, so long that Micah feared that he wasn't going to answer, before he said, "Quiet."

"Oh, yes," Micah said. "I suppose there aren't many people to talk to."

Terran looked up into the trees and said, "Things talk. Trees, animals, birds, but they just come to me with their worries, concerns. Not many conversations that can be had, y'know."

"Sounds lonely," Micah said, then immediately regretted it.

"'Tis, sometimes," Terran agreed.

There was a long silence between them then. Micah watched the water trickle over the stones in the stream. A frog hopped into the water, splashing gently. He tried to imagine it, being alone with just the beasts to speak to, just the trees. In a way, he could. The months when he first left Steephall, when his voice was still returning as his throat healed and he spoke only to Wilbur and only in broken sentences, hugging the donkey's neck as tears streamed down his face. Micah looked up at Terran.

"But now you will visit?" Terran asked.

Micah nodded, adamantly, and said, "Of course, at least once a week. I promise."

A grin spread across Terran's face as he said, "I'm glad."

MICAH KEPT HIS PROMISE. TERRAN WAS DISAPPOINTED AT FIRST that the cookies wouldn't make an appearance every week, only during market weeks. When Micah did bring cookies, Terran was ecstatic. He would take Micah's hands and squeeze them, and he always insisted that there was magic in them.

Spring turned to summer turned to autumn and Micah came every week bringing offerings. Each time, Terran would somehow be even bolder than before, laying a hand on Micah's shoulder or even the small of his back. He would lean down and whisper things in Micah's ear, sending shivers down his spine.

Sometimes, when Micah was working out in his garden or feeding the hens, he would feel eyes on him and sure enough, Terran would be there at the tree line. Micah always went over and visited with him for an hour or two before one of them had to get back to work.

Micah would sit in the shade at the edge of the forest, braiding grass together as Terran sat beside him, talking to him about the goings-on of the forest. Micah occasionally told him of the town, and Terran learned the names Marion and Kay as friends of Micah's as time continued to pass. Once, Micah brought over Wilbur and Terran bowed deeply to the donkey as though he were royalty.

"I can tell that you are a dear, old friend," Terran said, a smile on his face. "I'm glad he had someone he could talk to, even if he didn't understand your response."

"You can understand him?" Micah said, stroking Wilbur's neck and staring at Terran intently.

"Oh, yes," Terran said as Wilbur snorted.

"What is he saying? Micah asked, softly.

"He says he's glad to see you smiling again," Terran said, stroking the donkey's nose. "That you were sad for far too long."

When Micah broke away from Terran, leading Wilbur back to his favorite spot in the garden, he hugged Wilbur's neck. He whispered a thank you, again, and brought him a couple of carrots with his feed that night.

As he visited more and more, Terran took him deeper into the forest each time, talking with him about everything in the wood. Micah listened with rapt attention. Terran would take Micah's hand and place it on the rough bark of a tree, telling him its story in careful detail. Micah would listen, closing his eyes and feeling that deep history sinking into his skin.

Micah remembered with stark clarity the first time that Terran actually said his name. It was a warm summer day and they were walking through the forest. Micah was glad to escape the heat of the sun under the cool branches of the trees. Terran had promised him a cool, beautiful spring that he could bathe in if he wanted to. Micah had declined, laughing, and Terran seemed rather disappointed. But as they followed the stream, Terran suddenly stopped and took Micah's arm.

"Micah, look," he said.

Micah had followed Terran's pointing finger up to a bird that had an odd, golden coloration. It was striking, but Micah felt frozen. *You said my name. Say it again.* He fought the urge to shake his head at the silly thought.

It wasn't until another day, a few weeks later, that they made it to the spring. It was an incredibly warm day, even under the cover of the trees. Micah had shucked off his boots and stockings and rolled up his pant legs to dip his feet in the water. It was cool and refreshing, exactly what Terran had promised. There was a ledge where he sat, the clean gray stone smooth as it dipped down into surprisingly deep, clear water. He was kicking his feet and watching the ripples when a shadow flew over him and dropped into the water with an enormous splash.

Micah lifted his arms, blocking the spray, then looked behind him, horrified when he saw Terran's clothes shed in a careless pile. A red flush crept up his face as he turned to watch Terran emerging from the water, pushing his hair back from his face and showing off his well-toned body as droplets of water rolled off his face, neck, chest, arms… His hair was wet with the cool water and hung dripping onto his shoulders. More water clung to Terran's antlers, the droplets catching the sunlight like dazzling gems. The necklace that Micah had given him rested against his chest among curling hairs. He smiled over at Micah, boring into him with those bright green eyes.

"Want to join me?" he asked. "You look warm, the spring is quite cool."

Micah squawked unattractively and stumbled through saying, "Ah, I just don't want to get my clothes wet, they'll take so long to dry."

Terran moved closer to him—Micah tried not to look down through the clear spring—and said, "There's a very easy solution to *that*, my dear friend."

Micah let out a surprised laugh and looked up into the foliage above the spring, sure that he was redder than a ripe strawberry. He took off his hat and fanned his face with it carefully before setting it to his side. Two strong hands grabbed his ankles and he looked down to see Terran with a mischievous smile plastered on his face.

"Terran," Micah said warningly.

"Micah," Terran said, mimicking his tone.

That kept Micah from saying anything further, and Terran tugged him into the water with a thunderous splash. Micah emerged sputtering and coughing, his white shirt soaked and clinging to his body. He was sure his resurfacing was nowhere near as smooth as

Terran's had been, or as captivating, but Terran was gazing at him, enraptured.

"Well, there goes that," Micah said when he stopped coughing.

"Apologies," Terran said, still laughing. "I thought we were playing a game."

Micah couldn't help smiling at him, but he shook his head and said, "At least my hat is dry."

Terran reached out and brushed Micah's soaking curls out of his face with a grin. "Can't ruin the hat, now, can we?"

Micah laughed and said, "The hat is delicate! And it's very useful for someone like me who burns in the sun. The sun hates me."

"Now that is untrue!" Terran said, gently tapping a few of the freckles in the spray across Micah's nose. "She's given you so many little kisses."

Micah laughed and said, "That's the first time I've ever heard that. The sun is kissing me?"

"Sweet as honey, no wonder she wants to kiss you, see what you taste like," Terran said, licking his lips. "And she's not the only one."

Terran surprised him then—he was always surprising him—by pulling him closer, running a hand from his shoulder down to the small of his back, then cupping his face in his other hand. Terran smiled gently, then leaned in and kissed Micah. Micah's eyes widened for a moment before he closed them and let himself melt into it. When Terran pulled back, Micah gasped.

"Was that all right?" Terran asked, and for the first time Micah saw uncertainty in his face.

Micah nodded, unable to form words, and Terran grinned before kissing him again. Micah tried to imagine what about him made Terran so interested. He wasn't interesting. Not in the slightest. And yet, from the moment they met, Terran watched every move that Micah made, he listened to each word that Micah said, he asked questions and actually wanted the answers. Every time Micah had walked into the forest since they met, he had been waiting for him eagerly. Now, those green eyes were fixed on Micah's face with pure want. Terran moved to pull Micah's shirt off and Micah broke away.

"Wait, wait," Micah said quietly. "No. Not that. Not yet."

Terran's hands fell away as he said, "Apologies, I should have asked."

He suddenly lifted Micah out of the water, setting him back on the ledge in the sun. Micah shivered as the chill of the spring sank into him. Terran folded his arms on the ledge beside him and rested his head, looking up at Micah and smiling.

Micah smiled back, then faltered before whispering, "I don't understand. Why me?"

"Is that really so surprising?" Terran said, lifting his eyebrows.

Micah shrugged and said, "A little. I'm nobody."

Terran snorted and said, "Hardly. You're quite the person, Micah, and I wouldn't waste my time with someone who was less than the best."

Micah blushed and reached up to his neck, running a finger across the now-faded scarring there and said, "I don't know about that."

"Well, you'll just have to take my word for it," Terran said, placing a hand just above Micah's knee, moving his thumb in small circles.

Micah smiled at him and was pulled back into the water far more gently. He didn't submerge. Instead, Terran held him firm and steady against himself. Micah wrapped his arms around Terran's large, solid shoulders, shuddering slightly in the coolness of the pool. Though he might have been shivering from Terran's touch. Terran began kissing again: this time he kissed Micah's freckles, across his face, making him giggle as he brushed past his nose, then over to his ear and down his neck. When he got to the smooth skin where Micah's neck reached his shoulder, he applied more pressure and Micah reached up and wound his fingers into Terran's hair, gasping.

When Micah left the forest that day, he had a couple of marks on his neck. The next time he spoke to Marion, he covered them with a scarf despite the summer heat. It was far more noticeable than the marks, of course, and Marion pulled it off of him as he sat down at her table.

"You're playing a dangerous game, young man," Marion said, shaking her head.

"He's kind," Micah said, knowing better than to lie to her.

"He's wild," Marion said, "and that means you can't predict how he'll act."

"Have you ever encountered a bear in the forest, Mrs. Beath?" Micah asked, rubbing his finger against one of the love bites.

Marion snorted and said, "No, I don't go into the woods."

Micah smiled and continued, "Bears are wild animals. They aren't friends, they aren't pets, but they are also predictable. I know how a bear is going to act. I can avoid them when they're dangerous, or let them pass when they're calm. A bear isn't going to hurt me without reason."

"And your guardian spirit is like a bear?"

"He's closer to a bear than a civilized man. In my experience, men who call themselves civilized can be far more dangerous than wild animals."

Marion was quiet for a moment. "That I can understand."

She left it alone after that, though she would give him concerned looks when he stumbled out of the woods closer to her house than his, disheveled and with a lovesick smile on his face. He'd look around for a moment, wave to her, then walk back into the forest to be brought back to his house instead.

One day in the fall, Micah was laying out apples on the altar and Terran appeared behind him like he always did. Micah pictured the bemused look on his face and shook his head with a chuckle. Suddenly, Terran wrapped his arms around Micah's middle and pulled him back to his chest before he could finish arranging his gift.

"You could just sit on the altar yourself and be the offering," Terran said into his ear. "That would be more than enough for me."

Heart racing, Micah said, "Come now, Terran."

Terran pressed a kiss to the soft skin beneath Micah's ear and said, "I mean it. I would protect you, provide for you, I would crown you with flowers and cherish you for as long as you lived."

Micah was quiet. It was tempting. To forget about the world

outside, to forget about his responsibilities and his hardships, to just have Terran and the forest.

"I can't," Micah said softly. "I have responsibilities. There's the hens, and Wilbur, and the market. My friends, and I'm saving up for a hive…I have a life out there that I can't leave."

He felt Terran's disappointment, a slight sag of his body, a nearly inaudible sigh, but Terran rumbled, "I understand."

He led him further into the forest that day, far more quiet than he usually was, until they were somewhere that Micah had never been. He had been sure that at this point that he had seen every inch of the forest, as big as it was.

It was a clearing of the softest green, even as autumn yellowed the grass and leaves outside of this grove and turned them brittle. Wildflowers were growing, dotting the soft carpet with a rainbow of colors. And, at the center, there grew an enormous yew tree. Its branches dipped down, creating a canopy that shaded the ground beneath. The tree's wood was twisted, but healthy and sturdy. Wind blew through the clearing and shook the needles, creating a melody.

"What is this?" Micah said, wonderstruck, as he placed a hand carefully on one dipping branch.

"The center of the wood," Terran said, looking up at the tree in reverence. "The heartwood, the soul of the forest."

Micah turned to him in shock. His mother had told him of the heartwood long ago. This was not meant for human eyes, this was a delicate place of magic and power. He shouldn't be here. And yet Terran had brought him directly here and was showing it to him as though it were a particularly interesting tree or stone.

"Terran…"

"Also, where I sleep," Terran said, tipping his head to the side and grinning with a crooked smile.

"Oh!" Micah exclaimed, dropping his hand from the branch.

Terran looked at Micah in confusion for a moment before his own eyes widened and he held up his hands saying, "Oh, no! That is not why I brought you here! Apologies!"

Micah laughed and said, "It's all right, Terran."

"I just wanted you to see it," Terran said, smiling and looping his arm around Micah's waist and moving closer to the tree itself. "You did this."

"Did what?" Micah asked, looking up at Terran's serious face.

"It was dying," Terran said quietly. "Starving, and I was too. Living on scraps and hope, while the town ate away at the trees. But then you came along."

Micah grew very still, once again shocked that Roseyard hadn't been providing offerings to the guardian spirit, and apparently had been making him sick. He looped his arm around Terran's waist and squeezed as he looked up at the boughs.

"I'm sorry that they abandoned you," Micah said softly.

"But then you came," Terran said, grinning. "Sweet as honey and pretty as a flower."

Micah smiled half-heartedly, but he still couldn't believe Roseyard had ignored their forest. He started forming a plan in his mind as Terran lifted his hat carefully from his head and hung it on a low branch. Terran held his face in his hands, rubbing his thumbs in small circles against Micah's cheeks. Micah placed his own hands over Terran's, feeling their cool roughness. Micah lifted himself on his toes and kissed Terran, and Terran deepened the kiss with vigor.

Micah closed his eyes but felt Terran gently bring him against the tree as he continued to press into his mouth. Terran's hands held him in place and Micah's mind went pleasantly blank, not worried about the work he'd need to do when he got back, not worried about money, not worried about anything but being here and being kissed. Terran's offer lingered in the back of his mind, and he thought of daring to indulge in it.

Terran broke away then, and Micah opened his eyes. The spirit's face was twisted in concern as he looked not at Micah's face, but at his throat where the jagged network of scars still showed. Micah covered them with his hand and looked away.

"Sorry," Micah said. "I know they're not very pretty."

"That's not…" Terran started, then stopped. He was rarely at a loss for words, but he seemed to struggle as he looked at Micah.

"People weren't always kind to me, not like you're kind to me," Micah said, simply. "I don't want to think about it right now."

"All right," Terran said, and smiled gently. "I'll be kind to you now."

Micah spent far longer in the woods than he meant to that day, letting Terran undress him under the boughs of the yew tree and join their bodies. When he stepped out of the forest, the cool autumn air biting at his oversensitive skin, Terran grabbed his wrist and stopped him for a moment. Micah turned back in confusion, only to see Terran staring at him with an intensity that he had never experienced.

"If anyone hurts you, in any way, they will face a wrath that they cannot fathom," Terran said, holding onto Micah as though for dear life.

"I think I'm safe," Micah said, smiling and lifting the hand that Terran held up. He twisted his wrist so that he could press a kiss to the back of Terran's hand and hummed.

Terran smiled and let Micah's wrist go and said, "My offer still stands, my sweet."

"I'll remember it," Micah said.

As he finished his chores quickly, the sun setting behind the trees turning the sky to gold and rust, he could still feel Terran lingering and watching him. Micah found himself wondering if he could start planting trees closer and closer to his cottage, if he could bring Terran to him. That night, he dreamt of the branches of the yew tree.

4

THE LESSON

MICAH DECIDED THAT HE WAS A FOOL AND HE WOULD TRY something foolish. The idea that Roseyard had a lumber business and did not pay tribute to the guardian had always sat ill with him. But now, having seen the soul of the forest, and the soul of Terran, it was even worse.

It was an overcast, gray day, but that wouldn't stop him. Micah marched into town, a rarity on a day with no market, and found where Kay lived. It was a run-down, bleak little shack with hastily-patched holes in the roof and cloth nailed over broken windows. Cold wind blew through the covering, shaking it, and Micah imagined that the inside must be freezing.

Micah knocked lightly on the door and waited, bouncing on his heels. He glanced around the street; nearly every little house here was like this. Beaten down and depressing, falling apart and ramshackle, it was an odd sight given that there was so much prosperity in the rest of the town.

The door creaked open a mere few inches and a single watery gray eye obscured by dull red hair peered out. Micah leaned to the side, then smiled and waved. Kay grumbled something, then opened the

38

door the rest of the way. She looked even more tired than usual, but nodded in what was her friendliest gesture.

"Hello, Mr. Harlow," she said. "Come to make good on what I owe you?"

"Oh, not quite," Micah said, smiling. "And Micah is just fine, as I've said."

"Right, I keep forgetting," Kay said, tucking her hair behind her ear. "Then to what do I owe the pleasure, Micah?"

"I was wondering if you could tell me where the lumber business is," Micah said, smiling.

Kay was quiet for a moment before she said, "I know you're not an idiot. You're a fool, but you're not stupid. You could have asked anyone, or figured out where it was on your own. What's your game here?"

"No game," Micah said. "I just figured I could kill two birds with one stone. Figure out where the lumber business is and give this to you before the next market."

He reached into his bag and drew out a jar full of sweet honey, purified specifically for helping with sore throats. He had made it just the way his mother always did, down to humming the same gentle song she sang as she spun it. He held it out to Kay with a smile on his face.

"I knew it," Kay said, squeezing her eyes shut and pinching the bridge of her nose. "I don't want your charity."

"It's not charity— I'm paying you for information," Micah said. "I'd also love to know who owns and operates the business and if they've been having any trouble."

"How did you know that?" Kay said, looking at him with furrowed brows. "The lumber from the forest has been cursed for years. The man who owns it, Markus Henderson, is up to his eyeballs in debt to Fenwick."

Ah, there it was again. Charles Fenwick's name made itself known all throughout town. Those who didn't owe him for one thing or another were few and far between. He was a man of great influence and great wealth, and the town of Roseyard bent to his whims. Well, most of it did.

Fenwick had asked Micah at every single market if he was interested in selling his land and every single time Micah had refused. At one point, he had even insisted on taking Micah to dinner after the market. At first, Micah had demurred, but Fenwick had persisted. He made his men watch over Wilbur and his cart while he took Micah to the tavern and bought a truly absurd amount of food and drink. He offered Micah at least ten times what he had paid for the land, and did so just as Micah was taking a drink of ale, making him choke and spit in surprise.

"I'm sorry," Micah said, coughing as the man offered him a handkerchief.

"No need to apologize," Fenwick said with a wicked grin. "I had awful timing."

"It is a very tempting offer," Micah said, patting his shirt free of the ale, "but I'm still not sure."

"Well, Mr. Harlow," Fenwick said, sighing dramatically, "I'm afraid I can't do much better than that. It really just is the ideal land for what I have in mind. I can't understand why Mrs. Beath sold it to you when she refused me all these years. What are you using it for?"

"I live in the cottage," Micah said. "I'll be using some of the land for an apiary once I'm more settled."

"Beekeeping! I suppose that makes sense, you with the honey and all," Fenwick said, then affected a practiced puzzled look. "Though I do wonder where you are getting the honey right now."

Luckily, Micah was saved from answering by a raucous bunch of drunken patrons knocking over a table and roaring out the lyrics to a folk song. Fenwick muttered something and stood up to go find the tavern keeper. Micah took the opportunity to make his excuses when Fenwick returned, promising to think on it.

Micah had avoided Fenwick since then, but his presence hovered over him and the rest of the town like a specter. His influence and power were impossible to escape. Micah had experienced men like Fenwick before, and it never ended well. He wasn't sure how long he would be able to hold him off.

He thanked Kay for the information and explained the medicinal honey. She stared at him, shaking her head with a mirthless laugh.

"Okay, Mr. Witch, if that's what you say," Kay huffed.

"Oh, I'm not a witch," Micah said with an easy grin.

Kay furrowed her brow, then said, "Are you sure about that?"

"I mean, I think I would know," Micah said, laughing with surprise.

"Your cookies, though," Kay said. "And the honey drops. You had to have put a spell or something on them. They tasted like more than just sweets, they tasted like memories, and the drops helped my throat like nothing ever has."

"I suppose I should take that as a compliment!" Micah said, but he shook his head and said, "Well, they are my mother's recipes. She was a hedgewitch, but not me. Maybe there's a bit of lingering magic, but it's certainly not mine. I'm just…me."

That earned him a look from her, but she accepted it with a sigh and gave him directions. Then he was off.

Micah walked through the streets of Roseyard with purpose, and often the citizens looked at him in surprise. He hadn't been in town except on market days—he really had been spending so much time in the woods. He winced at the realization; that had been a problem back in Steephall as well. People only knew them as the witch and her son who sold things at the market. They were friendly with people, but had no deep roots in the town. When his mother died, he had been so alone for those few years before his run-in with…Well, he hardly wanted to think about that now.

He made an effort to wave at people and greet them with a friendly 'good morning' and made a mental note to come into town more often. His roots couldn't be in the forest alone.

Soon he found his way to the building Kay had directed him to. A yard full of lumber surrounded the small cottage. A dirty sign reading Henderson Logging Company hung over a door, its green paint chipped. Micah strode up to it, hopped up the step, and knocked lightly.

He glanced out at the yard and saw about a dozen very tired-looking men organizing the piles, a meager amount of wood for as large and bountiful as he knew the forest to be. Even from where he stood, Micah could see the wood was of poor quality, much of it rotted or eaten through by worms. A few of them made eye contact with him. Most he hadn't seen at the market, but he still offered a smile. No one reciprocated.

The door swung open and a man as short as Micah with a round, worn out face looked back at him. The man was likely in his forties, but life had taken a heavy toll on him. His face sagged, large bags dented the skin under his eyes, and his mouth seemed in a permanent frown. His hair must have once been a dusty brown, but it was more gray than colored at this point, as though the life had been sapped out of it.

"Can I help you?" the man, presumably Markus Henderson, asked in a long, drawn-out drawl that sounded as though he had neither the capacity nor desire to help himself, let alone anyone else.

"Good morning!" Micah said, smiling. "I don't know if you know me. I'm Micah Harlow. I'm fairly new to Roseyard."

"Oh, yes," Henderson said, rubbing the back of his neck. "You sell cookies. My daughter loves those."

"Oh, I'm glad to hear it," Micah said cheerfully, and then after a small moment he added, "May I come in?"

"I suppose," Henderson said, looking tired and dejected. "What is this about?"

Henderson moved out of the way to let Micah in, slinking into an office that was as gray and dusty within as the lumberyard was outside. The windows were caked with dirt on both sides of the panes, letting no natural light in, leaving Henderson to rely on a couple of oil lamps that gave the room a hazy, musty aura. Papers and ledgers were scattered all over the room, and Henderson sat heavily behind his desk, hiding behind the stacks of records.

"Hopefully, I'll be able to be of some help to you," Micah said, taking off his hat as he closed the door behind him.

He moved in and gingerly picked up a pile of papers from a beautifully carved, if ill-cared-for, chair. He sat, crossed his legs, and balanced his straw hat on his knee. He smiled warmly at Henderson, who stared at him in return.

"I don't mean to be rude, Mr. Harlow, but I don't really

understand how a baker could be of any help to me," Henderson said, rubbing his eyes.

"Call me Micah, please," Micah said, holding up a hand. "And the thing I may be able to help with is the forest. I understand that you've been having some trouble getting healthy lumber."

"How did you—" Henderson started, but then shook his head. "I suppose it's common knowledge. Yes, and if you are going to offer to loan me money, I don't want it. I have already borrowed far more than I can afford to."

"Oh no, "Micah said with a light laugh. "I couldn't offer to loan you money even if I wanted to. No, it's that I am rather experienced with forests. And pretty familiar with this one."

"This one?" Henderson asked, his brow furrowing.

"Yes," Micah said, hoping that Marion was mistaken about how strongly people felt about the forest. "I go in there to forage, to gather supplies, and many of the things I make and sell at the market are only possible because of the forest. And I always have a plentiful bounty."

"Well, bully for you," Henderson said, slumping back in his chair. "This forest hates me, I think."

"You're not wrong," Micah said with a shrug.

"I'm not wrong?" Henderson said, confusion dancing across his features. "What the hell do you mean by that, Mr. Harlow?"

Micah took a breath and said, "Look, it seems that a lot of the old ways have been lost here in Roseyard. It happens, I understand. But, you know, they were practiced for a reason. Have you made any offerings to the guardian spirit of the forest?"

"Have I done what?" Henderson sat up now, leaning forward and making Micah wonder if he had made a dire mistake.

"My mother taught me that whenever you go to forage, or to chop lumber, or to hunt, to take from the forest in any way, you need to give something to the forest in return," Micah said and then, seeing the skepticism on Henderson's face, quickly continued, "It doesn't need to be anything big. I can show you how to make an altar, and then you just have each of your men bring something that can't be found in the forest and leave it there. Then you can walk away, do your foraging—or logging in your case. It'll be gone when you come back and your bounty will be good."

"So, animals will eat what we leave," Henderson said.

"No," Micah said, folding his hands. "Though guardian spirits can take any shape, this one looks like a man. And it doesn't have to be food! I've left all kinds of things. The important thing is that it's an exchange, you know."

"Right," Henderson said. "And this…spirit is angry with me because I haven't been leaving him anything."

"Well, maybe not *angry*," Micah said. "But certainly disappointed. He feels disrespected, unwanted. And then you're not getting back his best in return."

Henderson grew silent, looking at Micah like he was only slightly mad and could be indulged. Not mad enough to be dangerous, luckily. Micah gave him his best smile.

"Look, it won't hurt to try it, right?" Micah said. "If it doesn't work, you're only out some meager offerings. If it does, well, it can really benefit you."

"It could cost the respect of my men," Henderson said, but he was rubbing his chin, warming to the idea.

"I'll take all the blame," Micah said. "You can tell them it was all my idea and you're just trying it. I have to show you how to make the offering anyway."

Henderson mulled it over, chewing on the notion like it was a particularly odd piece of meat in a stew, until he finally said, "All right."

"Oh, wonderful!" Micah jumped to his feet and grinned. "I'll come tomorrow morning, bright and early, yes? Tell the men to each bring something to offer, not of the forest."

"That seems simple enough," Henderson said.

"Oh!" Micah said, remembering. "Sorry, nothing with iron. Iron is poison to guardian spirits. Something about it hurts their magic."

Henderson nodded and Micah practically skipped out of the office. If this worked, then Terran would be well fed, the forest would be healthy, and Roseyard would be better off as well. Nothing but good could come from this and Micah was practically buzzing as he walked from the lumberyard.

MICAH STOPPED IN THE SHOPPING DISTRICT, LOOKING FOR something that he could offer Terran tomorrow. *That would be more than enough for me.* A pleasurable shiver ran down his spine, but he fought it off. He would certainly not offer himself on an altar with a crew of lumberjacks watching him.

He was chuckling to himself as he walked into the intriguing little trinket shop that always seemed to be closed on market days. It held an impossible amalgamation of junk and antiques, and Micah was drawn to it like a moth to flame.

The walls were covered in overloaded shelves, and the center of the room held freestanding cabinets that contained even more trinkets. Every inch of space was covered with some little knickknack or another. Statuettes made of precious stone or wood or metal, jewelry that ranged from priceless to children's playthings, books and hats and paintings and silverware and charms and crystals and…It was overwhelming, to say the least.

"Can I help you find something?"

Micah looked over to the source of the voice and saw an impossibly small old woman who in truth seemed more colorful scarf than woman. More than a dozen scarves enveloped her in a cacophony of hues and designs: Mismatched patterns covered her shoulders, bright sunset orange and red stripes beside a more subdued brown with white diamonds topped by looping yellow designs on green. The crowning touch was a vivid blue cloth dotted with stars holding back her hair. Micah smiled and tipped his hat to her.

"Hello there! Yes, in fact, I would absolutely adore some help," Micah said, moving closer to the scarf woman. "I'm looking for a gift for a…very dear friend."

The scarf woman looked him up and down, sniffed, and said, "Something for a lover, then? Tell me about him."

"Oh, I, er, that is, um." Sounds tumbled from Micah's lips as he turned bright red and the woman shuffled past him unperturbed.

"I'm too old to be beating around the bush, boy," she creaked. "Just tell me."

"He likes trees and animals," Micah said, feeling compelled as if by a spell. "He loves everything about the natural world, and sees all the beauty there, and…"

Micah cut himself off before he said something he regretted, and the old woman looked at him once more, assessing. Her eyes squinted behind owlish spectacles and she clucked her tongue before she held up a finger in triumph.

She scurried over to a particular shelf and climbed a set of wooden steps Micah had not noticed before that were built into the wall. She shot an age-spotted arm out from within the scarves and started expertly digging through the tchotchkes. Micah watched in awe as she revealed a small wooden stag with antlers that reminded Micah so much of the ones that grew from Terran's head. The woman handed it down to him and Micah took it with reverence.

It was a deep, dark brown, as hard as stone but warm to the touch and grained like wood, though not any type he had ever seen.. He rubbed his thumb against the beautifully carved flank of the deer and his fingers over the antlers. He imagined Terran doing the same and smiled.

"I'll take it," Micah said softly.

"I thought you would," the scarf woman said, descending the steps with a thump. "It'll be two silver."

Micah happily paid the price and thanked the woman for her help. She brushed him off, but told him to come again anytime. Micah stepped out into the street, placing the deer safely in his pocket, grinning from ear to ear. He needed to hum and mentally sorted through his mother's songs for just the right one. As he turned a corner, walking too fast, he was knocked suddenly to the ground as he ran directly into the large, imposing figure of Charles Fenwick, also moving rather quickly.

His hat went flying as his back hit the cobblestones and the air was knocked out of his chest. He twisted his hips as he fell to the ground so he wouldn't crush the little deer. He landed hard, but it would only leave a bruise. His bag had been flung to the side and a small jar of honey rolled out on the cobblestones, stopping at Fenwick's feet.

The big man reached down and picked it up and said, "Oh, drat, I do apologize, Mr. Harlow! I did not see you coming, allow me."

Micah was already starting to stand up, but Fenwick grabbed his arm and roughly yanked him upwards. Micah dangled for a moment that seemed like an eternity, his feet scrambling above the ground. Fenwick looked at him with vicious hunger and cruel delight, like an enormous house cat holding a mouse by its tail. Then Micah was set back on the earth and a large hand brushed the dirt off his back.

Micah was so stunned that it took until that moment to realize that he hadn't said anything and he quickly amended that. "It's quite all right, I should have been looking where I was going. My apologies to you, Mr. Fenwick."

Fenwick smiled his enormous wolf grin at Micah and swooped down to pick up the fallen straw hat. He held it delicately in his hands for a moment, then tossed it to Micah, who scrambled to catch it. He held it to his chest and watched as Fenwick pocketed the small jar of honey. At that, Micah had no idea what to say. Had that really happened? He blinked firmly a few times, then Fenwick cleared his throat.

"Well, fortuitous that I ran into you, Mr. Harlow," Fenwick said, catching Micah's eye. "It's not often that you grace us with your presence in town and it's a bit of a trek out to your cottage. I'm glad I don't have to wait until the next market day."

"Oh, yes," Micah said, wincing at another reminder of his absence from town. "Just had some business in town, you know. Pleasure seeing you as well."

He made to leave, but Fenwick caught his shoulder in a vise grip. Micah froze, the scars on his throat itching. Fenwick turned Micah back to him and stared him dead in the eye. There was something darker in there now, something Micah found uncomfortably familiar. He swallowed and his throat flared in pain.

"That was rather rude, Mr. Harlow," Fenwick said, his voice almost a growl. "I was speaking to you. I thought you were rather well-mannered, but it appears you need a lesson in courtesy."

Micah exhaled, sure that his fear was painted on his face in obvious strokes. "I am quite sorry, sir. I forgot myself. Please, excuse my rudeness. My mother taught me better."

Fenwick's hand on his shoulder immediately loosened and his face went back to being only slightly predatory as he said, "I quite say that she did! Anyway, I have something I'd like to discuss with you."

"Ah," Micah said, barricading his mind against another barrage of offers. "What can I help you with?"

"See, I have heard that Mrs. Beath is terribly ill," Fenwick said, his eyes gleaming. "An awful thing when one is so old, very dangerous."

The hair on the back of Micah's neck was standing on end; he didn't like the way Fenwick had told him that. The dance had begun, and he knew that he would have to step very carefully. One wrong move could break something vital and delicate.

"I am very sorry to hear that," Micah said. "She was her normal hearty self when I last saw her, but illness can strike hard and fast, as we know."

"Indeed," Fenwick nodded, wearing a mask of concern that would be appropriate for the situation if he actually cared. "I am curious: if she happens to pass, you will be quite lonely out there. Very isolated. It seems to me as though you would like to be closer to people. Living alone is always quite dangerous, you know."

"Yes," Micah said, and added, "Though living alongside certain people can also be quite dangerous." He winced at his daring.

"I'm not sure I catch your meaning, Mr. Harlow," Fenwick said, tongue flicking out like a snake's and wetting his lips. "What are you saying? Say it plainly."

Micah sighed and said, "I appreciate your offer, Mr. Fenwick, but I am simply not planning on selling my land. I am building my home out there. I would not want you to waste more of your very valuable time trying to persuade me."

Then the mask cracked and fell away, revealing primal anger, a hunger, a desire to rip prey limb from limb and rise bloody-mawed and howling. Fenwick's eyes betrayed him and his teeth looked sharp.

The air almost tasted of iron. Then the moment was gone and Charles Fenwick was wearing a disappointed but courteous smile.

"Well, no one could say that I didn't try!" Fenwick said, smiling. "Do check on Mrs. Beath for me, would you? I have a tender heart when it comes to old women."

Micah nodded, promising that he would, then got away from Fenwick as quickly as possible. The whole trip home his heart pounded in his ears. His hand wandered to the wooden deer in his pocket, stroking the antlers. What he really wanted to do in that moment was take Terran up on his offer, to live with him in his woods, but he thought of Wilbur and the hens, of Marion and Kay, of the lumber workers he had just promised to help, and shook his head.

He stopped by Marion's place that night and she was right as rain. He told her about his encounter with Fenwick, which made her spitting mad. She told him not to let Fenwick push him around, but that was truly easier said than done when it came to a man with so much power.

When he got back home—he was thinking of it as home now, wasn't he—he fed the chickens and Wilbur. Then, as he often did in distress, he wrapped his arms around Wilbur's neck and spoke to him, telling him all that had happened. The warm hair and steady breathing of the donkey always calmed Micah, and Wilbur knew he would get an extra carrot that night for being so good.

THE NEXT MORNING, MICAH ROSE BRIGHT AND EARLY, THE unpleasantness of the day before tucked away to worry about later, and he quickly made his way to Henderson's Lumber Yard. The men were standing about awkwardly, axes over their shoulders or at their sides, but also holding trinkets or bottles of milk or rolls of bread. The oxen were hitched up to the cart and ready to go, and Henderson, looking pale and nervous, hurriedly motioned Micah over when he smiled and waved cheerfully.

"The men are as desperate as I am, evidently," Henderson said, his voice falling to a hoarse whisper. "Willing to try just about anything. Are you sure this will work?"

"Absolutely," Micah said. "You have my word."

Henderson was nervously picking at his own felt hat, held in his hands, but he nodded at Micah. Micah gave the men a similar speech to the one he had given Henderson the day before. Many were just as skeptical as Henderson had been, but he saw some looks of recognition, especially in the faces of the older men, ones more likely to have heard of the old ways. Micah examined each of their offerings for iron, finding a set of utensils that he rejected, and led the men to the forest.

Micah had never entered the forest from this side, and he briefly worried that Terran would step out from behind some tree and look at him with confusion, sending the folks from Roseyard fleeing in terror. But he must have been able to sense Micah asking him to wait, to stay back, promising that he'd be back to visit him soon enough.

Micah led them carefully through the trees, staying mostly on the beaten trail, but he often found his feet wandering off deeper into the forest of their own volition. Not far inside, however, he perked up. Here was a perfect spot for an altar, right off the path. He motioned for the men to follow him and showed them how to set up the altar, arranging the rocks just so, crowning it with heather, and leaving space for the offering.

He pulled out a candle and set it in the center, saying, "Once all the offerings are within, you should light the candle and someone should say out loud that this is an offering for the guardian spirit of these woods."

"Is there a specific prayer or something?" asked a man who had been watching very carefully.

"Not really. As long as you offer it, it should be fine," Micah said, smiling at him. "I'll leave my offering, then I'll let all of you do the same."

He reached into his pocket and pulled out the small carved stag. He carefully set it next to the candle and smiled. He stood up and took a step back, the lumberjacks clearing a path for him, then he gestured for them to do the same. One by one, they did so. Bottles of milk, eggs, cheese, hard sugar candy, a scarf, a silver ring. Soon the altar was full.

"I think you should do the honors, Mr. Henderson," Micah said, handing him the flint.

"I suppose," Henderson said, taking it and pushing his hand through graying hair.

It took Henderson three tries to successfully spark the flint enough to light the candle, then he stumbled through a prayer, constantly looking at Micah for encouragement. Eventually, he finished and looked at Micah with raised eyebrows.

"And now what?" he asked.

"You go, cut down your trees, take your bounty," Micah said. "I bet you'll see a difference."

"All right, then," Henderson said, standing and brushing off his knees.

The men went to work, Henderson trailing behind them, looking back occasionally at Micah standing by the altar. Micah waited for a moment, looking down at the offerings with a smile. The candle had burned long enough, so he bent down and blew it out. Then he turned and walked out of the woods. He might have felt eyes watching him, but he didn't turn around, just smiled to himself.

Micah went back home for a while, taking care of the hens, who were very put out, and Wilbur, who was more forgiving. He cleaned the cottage and worked in the garden, smirking to himself when he felt eager eyes on him from the forest. And in the late afternoon, he walked over to Marion's and exchanged eggs for milk, and then, after dropping the bottle off at his house, made his way back to town and to the lumberyard.

He grinned when he saw the expressions on the men's faces. The lumber was healthy, and there was so much of it. It was being sorted, and the men all seemed light on their feet despite the exhaustion they should have been feeling. When Henderson spotted him, he rushed over.

"Mr. Henderson! How did it—whoa!" Micah was cut off as Henderson wrapped him in an unexpected hug.

He actually lifted Micah off his feet and squeezed the breath out of him, laughing joyfully. He eventually set Micah down and looked horribly embarrassed, reaching up and fixing Micah's hat for him.

"Apologies, Mr. Harlow, Micah," Henderson said. "I just can't tell you…We've never had a day like that. No trouble at all! Every tree fell the way it should, no unexpected rot, no injuries…This was a blessing."

Micah grinned and said, "I'm so pleased."

"And we just need to offer those little things each time?" Henderson asked, and after Micah's enthusiastic nod, he added, "What can I do to repay you?"

"Oh, no need!" Micah said, lifting his hands. "Just remember to honor the guardian spirit."

"I just don't understand what you get out of this," Henderson said, rubbing the back of his neck.

"Well, I go into the forest quite a bit myself," Micah said, tilting his head with a sly smile. "I have a vested interest in keeping the guardian happy."

It wasn't a lie, and Henderson accepted it, shaking Micah's hand and returning to the men. Micah looked on happily, then headed home.

5

———————

THE GIFT

T{HE NEXT TIME} M{ICAH WENT INTO THE WOODS, JUST A FEW DAYS} after he taught Henderson how to make an offering, he didn't make it three steps before Terran was upon him. Terran wrapped his arms around Micah from behind and lifted him up, spinning him around while laughing like thunder. Micah was only momentarily shocked before he joined in, his own laughter high and light among the trees. When Terran finally set him down, Micah was so dizzy that he couldn't see straight.

Terran turned him around and kissed him, saying against his mouth, "You are an absolute wonder, Micah! A gift to this world. Whatever would I do without you?"

When he released Micah, who was dazed on several accounts, Terran looked at him with a smile that warmed him even on this frigid fall day. Terran's hands were cupping his face, and his thumbs made little circles against his cheeks. Micah's hat had flown off, landing somewhere among the trees, and Terran leaned down, pressing a gentle kiss to Micah's forehead.

"I'm glad you're happy," Micah said, his voice soft.

"Happy is hardly the right word, 'tis too small for what I feel,"

53

Terran said. "I cannot believe that I have someone like you, someone who cares so deeply. I don't know what I did to deserve it."

Micah just smiled and pulled one of Terran's hands from his face to press a kiss to his fingers. Terran looked at Micah as though he were the only person in the world.

"Come on," Terran said, whispering in Micah's ear. "I saw that you offered something to me, and yet you took nothing from the forest."

"Oh, I have an offering for you today," Micah said, starting to reach into his bag.

Terran grabbed his wrist to stop him, then lifted Micah's chin with his finger as he said, "Don't you understand? I don't need any offerings from you, Micah. You can take freely, you have already given me so much. Your being here is enough offering from you."

"Oh," Micah said, his eyes widening.

"I've already told you this, my sweet," Terran said, a lopsided grin on his face. "Please, let this be a gift to you."

Micah swallowed, smiled, and then, with an impossible amount of effort, he said, "All right. Thank you."

Terran hunted down Micah's hat and placed it back on his head with a grin. Micah adjusted it and thought to himself that he really ought to lace a cord through it to keep it in place.

Terran took Micah's hand and, as he had done so many times, led Micah into the forest. This time, though, they did not even slow down as they passed the altar. They only paused a few times for Terran to press Micah against a tree and kiss his lips, or his neck, or slip his hands under Micah's shirt until Micah giggled and told him to wait.

"Apologies, apologies," Terran murmured in his ear. "Later?"

Micah found himself grinning and saying, "All right, later."

Terran took him to the grand yew tree at the center of the forest again. It looked even more alive, somehow. Its beauty nearly took his breath away, but Terran stole it completely when he took Micah's hand and suddenly spun him around like a dancer. He dipped him so that his hat, once again, fell from his head, letting his blond curls dangle mere inches from the ground. Micah looked up at Terran, who was looking down at him with his wild green eyes, somehow softer in this light.

"That was unexpected," Micah said, and then Terran pulled him back up, moving them into a dancing position, his hand on Micah's waist, Micah's hand on Terran's shoulder, and Terran holding their free hands together.

"Do you dance?" Terran asked, a soft, warm note in his voice.

"Not well," Micah said. "Sorry if I step on your toes."

Terran swung him around, moving to his own soft humming. The steps seemed practiced, and Terran was a good dancer. His body moved with a secret rhythm, and he pulled Micah along with him.

"I used to dance all the time," Terran said. "Before…"

Terran suddenly stopped, brow furrowing, and he appeared to be holding something back, like a beaver's dam containing the rushing river. Terran dropped Micah's hand and smiled, but there was a new sadness in his eyes.

Micah bit his lip and then, after a kiss to Terran's cheek, he ventured, "Before?"

Terran rarely hesitated, but he did now. He held his breath for a moment, then moved over to the yew tree. He sat down, leaning his back against the rough bark. He motioned for Micah to join him and Micah scurried over, nearly tripping on the exposed roots. Terran smiled, but it didn't reach his eyes. Micah sat down next to him and leaned his head against Terran's shoulder.

"Do you know how guardian spirits are made, Micah?" Terran asked, his voice the softest Micah had ever heard it.

Micah realized that he had never really thought about it. He had assumed that guardian spirits just *were*. That they had always been there. Apparently, he was wrong. He shook his head.

"I was chosen," Terran said. "A long, long time ago. The forest chose me as its protector when it was young and new. The town wasn't called Roseyard then. It didn't really have a name. 'Twas just where some people lived together. I used to dance, I danced all the time. In the center of the village, on festival days, for people's weddings, and where I really went to dance was here."

He reached up and touched the trunk of the yew fondly, smiling, then he continued, "And the burgeoning forest liked it. I had come here many times, but this night…'twas different. I was angry, and hurt. I don't even remember the reason, to be quite honest. Some fight or another, maybe with a friend or a lover, but 'twas so long ago. I danced with such a passion that the forest reached out to me…it liked watching me dance. And it wanted to keep on watching me dance."

Terran looked up into the branches of the yew then, and Micah watched him blink back a few tears before he said, "It offered me a place, told me that as long as the yew, the heart of this forest, lived on, I would as well. I would be gifted with tools, magic of a kind, that I could use to make the forest safe. I would always belong here."

"Terran," Micah said, moving to take Terran's wide hand in his.

"It didn't tell me how lonely it would be," Terran said softly. "I'm making you the same offer, but I want you to know that this is such a long, long time. I don't want you to do it unless you want to. I know…I know you've considered it."

Micah swallowed and nodded.

"Even if you're only here for now," Terran said, turning to face Micah. "I'm glad. You have been a sweet gift in a barren land."

Micah didn't know what to say, couldn't bring himself to say anything, so instead he kissed Terran. The kisses he initiated had always been chaste up until now. But this time, when he pushed their mouths together, he tried to ground himself and Terran here in this moment, their teeth clacking together briefly. Micah slowly pulled back, Terran's bottom lip held gently between his teeth, before he let go.

"Anything," Terran said, his voice sounding broken and desperate. "Anything you want and it will be yours, a gift back for all you have given me, though it could never repay you."

"I don't want anything," Micah said, in between the kisses he was planting on Terran's neck. "Nothing, I just want you to be happy."

Terran stopped him then, placing his hands on Micah's face and pushing him back to look in his eyes. Terran's own were even more wild than usual as he searched Micah's flushed face. He wove his fingers into Micah's curls and smiled.

"I'm already happy," Terran said. "I suppose I'll just have to figure out something for you myself. After all, I never gave you anything for the deer."

Micah laughed lightly and shook his head, saying, "You don't have to…"

"Oh, but I do," Terran said, grinning and pulling Micah into his lap. "It'll be a poor example for the lumber workers if I did not, right?"

Micah let himself be pulled into Terran again, and didn't emerge from the woods until well after dark. Terran stood at the tree line, watching him and making sure that he made the short trip to his cottage safely.

He took care of the very disconcerted hens and Wilbur, who snuffled his ear and pulled his straw hat off his head, making Micah giggle. Before he stepped inside the cottage, he lifted a hand to Terran, and he swore he could see that Terran was waving back.

A WEEK LATER, HE STEPPED OUT OF THE COTTAGE, AND AS HE WAS about to take care of the hens, he spotted a strange shape at the edge of the forest. Then he heard a sound, a sound that filled his heart as much as his ears. Buzzing.

Micah rushed over to the forest's edge, not believing it at first, but there it was. Dripping with golden honey and surrounded by sleepy, happy bees, it was a hive. Micah's hands shot up to cover his mouth, and then Terran stepped out from behind a tree, smiling at him.

"I hope you'll still come and visit me, though," he said, a lopsided grin on his face.

"Terran," Micah said. "Of course, but, you don't know what this means. It's…it's been too long."

Micah rushed over to Terran and wrapped his arms around him in a staggering hug. Terran stumbled back slightly, laughing, but wrapped his arms around Micah in turn. Micah didn't mean to cry, but tears streamed down his face and a small sob escaped from his lips. Terran pulled back and looked at him with utter concern.

"Are you all right?" Terran asked, searching Micah's face.

"Ah, yes, I'm sorry," Micah said, scrubbing his eyes with his fists. "It's just, my mother and I used to tend the hives together. Then after she died, after I was on my own, they were all that I had to remember her by. Then when I…they destroyed the apiary. Smashed the hives to pieces. The only things I truly have left of her are my hat and Wilbur."

Terran looked at him carefully, then gingerly laid a finger on Micah's scarred throat before he said, "Who are *they*?"

Micah shook his head. "It doesn't matter, they're a world away. And now I have you, everything is fine. Sorry, what I should be saying is thank you. Thank you, Terran."

Terran bent and pressed a kiss to Micah's cheek and said, "There's no need, Micah. This is my thank-you to you."

Micah would need to build a hutch, and luckily he knew exactly where to get lumber. He had to peel himself away from Terran, but he finished his morning chores, then hitched Wilbur up to his cart to head into town. He walked along the woods' edge, and Terran joined him occasionally, though there were times when he stepped away to take care of the forest.

When Micah walked into town, he noticed that the townsfolk seemed to recognize him and there were many smiles and waves. He reciprocated, but it puzzled him. It wasn't until he moved past the butcher's shop that he saw a familiar face with dull red hair and gray eyes as Kay rushed over to him.

"Good morning, Mr. Harlow," Kay said. In a more hushed tone she added, "You've become a legend, Micah."

"Oh, how so?"

"The lumber, you fool," Kay said with a laugh. "Everyone's talking about it. You worked your magic again. You've saved Henderson's business, which helped literally every person who works for him."

"Oh! Oh, wonderful!" Micah said, grinning. "I'm so glad. It wasn't actually magic, you know. But I am happy. I was actually on my way to see if I could buy some lumber from him."

"He's not going to let you," Kay said with a snort.

"Oh, why not? I should have enough coin," Micah said, his brow furrowing in confusion.

"He's not going to let you *pay* for it, Micah," Kay said. "The way he's talking, you hung the moon in the sky."

"Oh," Micah said, stunned. "I wasn't expecting…"

"What were you expecting?" Kay asked, arching a brow. "No one is that selfless, Micah."

"Oh, I definitely had an ulterior motive," Micah said with a laugh. "I am only human, after all."

"And that was?"

"I get my livelihood from the forest, and the forest wasn't happy with the loggers. A happy forest makes my life easier, and happier as well. See? Purely selfish."

Kay narrowed her eyes. Micah could tell that she knew he was holding something back. She let it drop, though, and continued to walk beside him, nodding at residents who cheerfully waved at him and completely dismissed her. He stroked Wilbur's neck a few times and Wilbur snuffled Micah's neck in turn, knocking his hat to the ground.

Kay swooped down and picked it up, offering it to him and saying, "No offense intended, but that hat has seen better days. Why not get a new one? This one doesn't seem to fit you very well. It's on the ground half the time that you're 'wearing' it."

Micah laughed and took the hat, saying, "Thank you, and well, there are a lot of memories attached to this hat. I'll wear it until it's literally falling apart."

As if on cue, a piece of straw dropped from the hat to the ground, which made both of them laugh. Even Wilbur snorted, appreciating the timing. Kay walked with Micah the rest of the way to the lumber yard before making her excuses and leaving him. It was a perfect autumn day, crisp and cool, with endless blue skies dotted with small, fluffy clouds.

The lumber yard was abuzz with far more activity than Micah was expecting. It was loud and busy, oxen tugging the logs to where they were being cut into smaller, more manageable pieces. Men with wagons and horses exchanging coin and bartering over prices, and at the center of it all was Henderson. His previous deflated self was gone. He was happy and boisterous, and when he saw Micah with his small donkey and cart, he rushed over.

Wilbur seemed to be puffing himself up in competition with the oxen nearby when Henderson strode up to Micah and slapped him heartily on the back, causing him to stumble slightly. Henderson patted Wilbur affectionately, then grinned at Micah.

"I cannot thank you enough! Look at this place—it hasn't been this way in generations." Henderson spoke every sentence with a loud, booming voice that Micah could hardly connect to the little, gray man that he had met before.

"I'm glad!" Micah said, grinning. "I was actually wondering if I could buy a bit of lumber from you. See, I just acquired a hive and I need to build a hutch…"

"I'll do you one better!" Henderson said, beaming. "I'll have one of my men build the hutch right now, send you home with it by the end of the day. And, of course, no cost."

"Oh, I couldn't possibly," Micah said, holding his hands up. He hadn't really believed what Kay had said about not having to pay.

"You can, and you will!" Henderson said, clasping his hand on Micah's shoulder. "It's a gift, from me to you. You gave us that lesson for free, and my wife would never let me hear the end of it if you didn't get a gift in return."

He couldn't help but think about what his mother always said: that good deeds will be paid back, that when you put kindness into the world, it will come back threefold to you. It certainly hadn't felt that way a year ago, but now he had Terran, and this kindness was coming back to him again.

Micah smiled helplessly and said, "Oh, all right. Thank you."

"Fantastic! Leave the donkey and cart here, they'll be well taken care of, I swear," Henderson said, once again patting Wilbur.

"Be on your best behavior, Wilbur," Micah said, stroking the donkey's nose. "When do you think you'll be done?"

"Late afternoon," Henderson said. "If you have work to do, I can always send one of the men out to your place with your cart."

"That might be for the best," Micah said cheerfully. "If it's not too much trouble, of course."

"No trouble at all!" Henderson replied and, once again, slapped Micah's back.

Micah headed out, Wilbur giving him a concerned look as he was left behind with the enthusiastic Mr. Henderson, and made his way back to the town center. He didn't really want to spend too much time here, as much as he liked to greet the other citizens. The vague shadow of Fenwick was still lingering in his mind as he strolled past a cart selling an odd little sugar treat in the shape of a deer. He stopped.

"How much for two?" Micah asked, looking at the little stags.

The teenager manning the cart looked up from the dice game he was playing and said, "Uh, it's three for five bits."

"Sounds great," Micah said, digging out the bits and handing them over to the bored boy.

The boy packed them up in a greased paper, looking perturbed that anyone had dared to purchase anything. He handed them over to Micah, and then a look of recognition passed over the boy's face.

"Oh! You're the cookie guy!" he said, brightening. "Though my sister would call you the soap guy. She goes to your booth every market day! I always get her to buy me a cookie. Or three."

"Oh! Well, thank you," Micah said, grinning. "I always appreciate a repeat customer."

"Yeah, no problem," the kid said and then, after a moment, asked, "You're new in town, right?"

"Fairly," Micah said. "I got here at the start of spring."

"So, you probably don't know about the candies," he said, grinning a mischievous grin and leaning forward conspiratorially. "See, Beast's Night is almost upon us."

"Beast's Night?" Micah asked, lifting an eyebrow.

"Yeah," the boy said, clearly pleased to have an audience. "See, on the last night of fall, everyone gets these candies. You give one to someone you care about, one to yourself, and then you leave one on the windowsill. For the beast! As long as your house has candy out for the beast, he won't come in and get you."

"Get me?" Micah asked, trying not to laugh.

"Yeah, well, eat you, tear you apart, I don't know exactly what the beast of the woods does," the boy said with a shrug. "But anyway, I don't want to find out. Supposedly, he has deer antlers, so he likes that they're shaped like deer. But other than that, he looks like a man."

"I see," Micah said, fighting a smile.

"Glad I was able to tell you," the kid said with a sage nod. "I wouldn't want you getting eaten up by the beast, we'd miss your cookies something fierce."

"I'm glad you told me as well," Micah said, nodding back, then after a moment, he asked, "When did this start?"

"Oh, years and years ago," the boy said, scratching at his pimply face. "Back when my great-granddad was a kid, I think. When Douglas Fenwick was the townhead."

"Douglas Fenwick?" Micah asked, brow furrowing.

"Yeah, Douglas Fenwick died a while back, but he had all sorts of things he did in Roseyard. There's a plaque by Charles Fenwick's house, you know. That was his grandad," the boy said with another sage nod. "They say that Douglas Fenwick did battle with the beast, you know."

"Oh," Micah said, eyes widening.

"Ah, don't worry," the boy said. "The candy keeps the beast away!"

"Right, thank you," Micah said, disconcerted all over again.

Micah turned and walked away before he could say something about it. He wanted to ask Terran about this; he wondered if he knew. He tucked the sugar deer into his bag and started to leave the square but was pinned in place by the glare of Charles Fenwick.

Micah cursed silently, wishing he had just walked past the booth, but there was nothing to do now. Fenwick stalked up to him, predatory as always, eyes roving up and down Micah's frame. He was looking particularly catlike today with a sneer that revealed teeth that, in the right light, looked almost as though they had been sharpened to a point.

"Mr. Harlow," Fenwick said as he closed in on him, his voice low and dangerous.

"Good morning to you, Mr. Fenwick," Micah said, smiling and keeping his voice bright.

"I've been hearing a lot about your exploits recently," Fenwick said, narrowing his eyes. "I heard that you gave some advice to Markus Henderson that has greatly paid off."

"Yes! I'm so pleased that it has," Micah said cheerfully. "Always happy to do someone a good turn."

"Indeed," Fenwick said. "He made the first payment on his debt in nearly a year. He was so relieved, you know. If he hadn't made a payment soon, I would have been within my rights to take his lumber yard as payment. Or perhaps his home."

"Well, quite lucky that I was able to give him that advice then," Micah said. "That could have been devastating."

"Quite lucky," Fenwick said, reaching to his finger and twisting the brass ring there. "Tell me, Mr. Harlow, where did you learn such a clever little trick?"

"Ah, well, my mother taught me," Micah said, smiling. "We were always sure to keep the old ways, you know. She and I kept bees while she was still alive, but we also foraged in the forest near the old town."

"And what town was that?" Fenwick asked.

Micah froze. From anyone else, the question would have been innocuous. But there was something in the timbre of Fenwick's voice, the gleam in his eye, that gave Micah pause. However, he could hardly lie or refuse to answer the question. Once again, he was caught like a mouse.

"Steephall," Micah said.

"Steephall," Fenwick repeated, as though he were committing it to memory. "Well, I hope you have a most pleasant day, Mr. Harlow of Steephall."

Fenwick turned and walked away. The moment he was gone, Micah's hand fluttered up to his scars. He wished he hadn't left Wilbur behind, as he wanted to wrap his arms around the steady beast's neck and feel grounded. Instead, he walked as if in a daze out of town and back to his home.

The cottage was the same as always, but it was as though a shadow had been cast over everything. He went to the hens and tended them, moved the hive closer to the house and made sure it was intact and safe, then worked mindlessly in the garden. At noon, his rumbling stomach shook him out of his listlessness.

He went inside, grabbing just some cheese and bread and a few late berries. After a moment, he grabbed more of everything and filled a woven basket. He flung a blanket over his shoulder and headed to the tree line, the sugar deer in their waxed paper sitting next to bottles full of cider.

He spread out the blanket just inside the trees and set the basket down. He sat down and leaned back on his elbows, tilting his head back to look at the canopy above and the light dappling through it. He watched a squirrel dance from branch to branch, tilting his head so far that his hat once again dropped to the forest floor. Eventually, he felt a presence next to him and looked over with a smile to see Terran sitting on the blanket.

"Hello again, my sweet," Terran said, leaning over Micah and grinning.

"Thought you might like some lunch," Micah said, smiling.

"Depends on what's for dessert," Terran said, cocking his head to the side.

"How did you—?" Micah started to ask before he realized what Terran meant. "Oh! Well, I suppose that we can do that too."

"I do call you sweet for a reason," Terran said, bending his neck to kiss Micah on the cheek. "But all right, lunch first."

After they ate, Micah telling Terran about everything that had happened in Roseyard with excited sweeps of his arms as they shared the cheese and bread, Micah unwrapped the little deer candies and told Terran the story that the seller had related to him.

"I guess you get two from me," Micah said with a smile, popping the candy into his mouth.

"I can't believe they're still doing that," Terran said with a laugh. "I don't even get the candy! I can't leave the woods!"

Micah laughed and, although he didn't want to ruin the mood, he also told Terran about the encounter with Fenwick. Terran's face grew still and serious, and he watched Micah carefully as he spoke. When Micah finished, Terran thought for a moment and then turned his head thoughtfully.

"I know that you don't want to talk about it," Terran said, and Micah tensed. "But what happened in Steephall?"

Micah's hand moved unbidden to the scars on his throat and then he said, "I don't know if I can tell you yet."

Terran's face twisted and he asked, "Why not?"

"It's not you," Micah said, shaking his head. "It's me. I don't think I can make myself tell it. It just…it still hurts too much."

Terran nodded, and added softly, "If Fenwick hurts you, I will do everything in my power to destroy him. You understand?"

Micah nodded but he forced himself to smile as he said, "Most of Fenwick's power comes from money. I don't think I have anything to worry about."

Terran placed the other sugar treat in his mouth, letting it melt as he looked deep into Micah's eyes. "As you say."

It was nearly sunset when a man arrived with the hutch pulled by a very perturbed Wilbur. Micah thanked him profusely and pushed a few cookies his way in payment, which the man took awkwardly before bidding him a good night.

Micah brushed down Wilbur and stabled him for the night. He probably should have waited until the next day to set up the hutch, but he couldn't. It was perfect. The hive fit inside like a hand in a glove, and he wasn't even stung. After it was snug, he sat on the ground in front of it, fighting back a few traitor tears, before looking back at the forest to where Terran stood. He waved, and his lover waved back.

The bees' buzzing filled his mind, his heart, his soul, with a deep and profound happiness that he had missed dearly. It wasn't that he hadn't been happy, but this...this felt like the last true piece of the puzzle to make this cottage his home. He smiled.

6

THE FIRE

Things were calm for a while. The Beast's Night celebrations came and went, the lumber yard flourished, and market days continued. Micah had gotten into a routine of coming to town once a week, even when it was not a market day. He decided that he would be a part of the community this time, and he found that he was. In fact, he was surprised to learn that he had quite a positive reputation in town, something that was foreign to him since his mother's death.

Marion grudgingly admitted that he had been right about the forest. She had seen him stumble out enough times, and had enough glimpses of Terran through the trees, by then to concede the point, something that, as far as Micah knew, was akin to a miracle. He had grinned as she went to the altar and left something for Terran, and then she smacked the back of his head for teasing an old woman.

Cold was setting in, and there was less and less reason for Micah to venture into the forest, but that hardly stopped him. He was among the trees nearly every day at this point, breathing in the crisp, sharp scent of the winter forest. Terran would appear and they would speak or walk or do a thousand other things to keep themselves entertained.

Even in the winter months, Terran strode through the forest

barefoot, wearing just the loose tan shirt and tattered pants. Snow covered the forest floor and it didn't even seem to bother him, though his toes sunk into the frost. Micah, however, was under no such magic. The cold still bit at his skin and made him shiver. When Micah wore a jacket and a sweater over his shirt, Terran grunted in frustration while trying to touch him.

"How many layers does one man need?" he asked as Micah erupted in laughter.

He had put away his straw hat and taken to wearing a knit cap and matching mittens that Marion made him out of brown yarn. As Micah laughed, Terran smirked and pulled the cap down over Micah's eyes, which just made him laugh so hard he stumbled into a tree. He pulled up the cap and grinned at Terran.

"Not all of us can go around barefoot in the snow, love," Micah said, fighting off his giggles. "And I don't want frostbite to take away anything important."

Terran suddenly froze, he looked at Micah very carefully and asked, "What did you just call me?"

It was Micah's turn to freeze. He hadn't even meant to say it. It had just slipped out of his mouth, as natural as could be. He hoped that he hadn't made a mistake, that he hadn't ruined it all. He swallowed and spoke.

"I called you 'love,'" he said, soft as the snow that was gathering on the branches above. "Is that all right?"

Terran was on him faster than Micah's eye could track. He wrapped an arm around Micah's waist, then pulled his cap off and ran his fingers gently through his hair. He pressed a kiss to Micah's forehead.

"Of course it's all right, my sweet," Terran said. "Of course."

The days carried on like that as the winter grew deeper and the air colder and the sun spent less and less time in the sky. Days spent in the forest or in town were often very short. Micah would wake in the morning and bring warm water out to the hens and Wilbur. He had wrapped the bees for the cold winter months and kept the hive close by. His garden had gone to sleep, but that didn't mean there was less to do. Keeping his woodpile stocked was a constant battle. Terran must have seen Micah's attempts at chopping wood and taken pity on him, because one day there was a neat, tidy pile of wood at the forest's edge.

ON ANOTHER DAY IN THE DEEPEST WINTER, WITH SNOW POURING from the sky and wind whipping around, when Micah knew that Terran would entirely understand his remaining shut up in the cottage, he heard an urgent knock on the door. Micah was puzzled; he had been outside not twenty minutes ago to take care of Wilbur and the hens, making sure that the garden and hive were covered. He hadn't seen anyone at all, and he was still defrosting by the fire. He went to the door and found a shivering, shaking Marion, her body wrapped under a mountain of blankets. Micah immediately pulled her inside.

"Marion! Did you walk all this way in that storm? Are you all right?" He moved her to the hearth, peeling back layers of wet blankets and then covering her in his own dry quilts.

"Roof collapsed, the snow must have done it," she said shakily.

"Oh," Micah said, wrapping an arm around her. "Oh, I'm so sorry. You're welcome to stay here, of course. Would you like some tea?"

Marion nodded, but her eyes were a thousand miles away. Micah bustled around making tea and then started on soup. He made sure that she wasn't injured and had no frostbite on her toes or finger tips before questioning her.

"Marion, what happened?" Micah asked in a soft whisper.

"I think he's finally won," Marion said with a sigh. "I can't afford to fix the roof. I'm going to have to sell my house and my land, my cows…I can go and live with my daughter over in Kipperfield, but this was my home."

"Who's won?" Micah asked, taking the finished tea cup from her hands and replacing it with a bowl of soup.

"Fenwick, of course," Marion said. "He's been after my land for ages. I've never given so much as an inch, and now here we are, the snow's gone and done the work for him."

Micah's blood went cold. Of course it was Fenwick. He didn't know why he wanted their land so badly, or the lumber yard either, for that matter, but he hungered for it like a wolf eyeing a ewe lamb. Micah tapped his fingers on the empty tea cup.

"Maybe I could ask Henderson and his men if they could cut a deal," Micah said. "It would cost a lot more than a hutch, but…"

"Don't you dare go into debt for me, young man," Marion said, eyes snapping up to him. "I am getting older and retiring is not a bad idea. I'm just angry that Fenwick is the only one in town who'd be able to afford my land. Promise me this, Mr. Harlow. Don't sell that man an inch. Hold it away from him, make him go hungry."

Micah crouched down so his eyes were even with hers and nodded, saying, "I promise. I wouldn't sell this land for a hundred times what it's worth."

Marion snorted and said, "Well, let's not be foolish…"

Micah laughed, then shook his head. "You know it's also for other reasons."

"Oh, I hate to admit when I'm wrong," Marion said with a rueful smile on her lips. "But I think I was with that one."

Micah just smiled and said, "You're free to stay here as long as you need, through the winter at least. I can come to town with you to speak to Fenwick, if you like."

Marion snorted again, and said, "Please, I can handle that old snake just fine. But I'll take you up on your offer of a roof all the same. I'll have to go over to my place to take care of the cows, though."

"I can do that," Micah said, smiling. "At least until they're sold."

"You give too much, Mr. Harlow," Marion said with a sigh. "What will you have left for yourself?"

"Micah, please," he said. "If you're going to be living with me, I must insist."

"Micah, then," Marion said. "Don't give too much of yourself away, dear."

Micah offered her another smile and then said, "I'd rather give a bit away to ease someone's pain than hoard it all up and end up like Ed—Fenwick."

If Marion caught his slip, she didn't show it. She smiled weakly and didn't press. As he cared for her that night, he wrapped blankets around her and hummed the song his mother would sing when he was sick. The song was about warmth and comfort, healing and hope, and love and safety. As Marion finally drifted to sleep beside the fire, Micah could have sworn that there was a bit more color in her cheeks and that she breathed a bit easier.

She stayed with him for the rest of the winter, and he imagined that this was what it was like to live with an old, grumpy barn cat confined inside the house after it could no longer kill mice. Marion was testy when she didn't have something to do, so she would often slap Micah's hands away from household chores and do them herself. It worked out, since he would trek to the barn at Marion's place each day to take care of her cows until a man in town bought them.

He spent a few long days gathering a list of things from Marion's ruined house, terrified of every creak and groan the structure gave while he was inside it. Soon, his small common area was half-filled with Marion's things. She was so indignant about putting him out that she went through his closet and mended each and every small bit of wear and tear in his clothes. She even rewove his straw hat. When he discovered this, she pushed away his thank-yous like a child refusing vegetables.

When Marion travelled into town to sell her land to Fenwick, Micah insisted on accompanying her. Although she was generally as unmovable as a stone embedded in the ground, she finally gave in and let him come along. He hitched Wilbur up to the cart and made Marion ride in it. At first, she was appalled, but eventually, she held her head high like a queen as the wheels bounced against the town's cobblestones. She gathered up her skirts and marched into Fenwick's place, not even knocking.

Micah stood outside in the cold winter air waiting for her, rubbing his hands together through the mittens and blowing out puffs of cloudy breath into the morning. Wilbur's little puffs of air joined his, and they looked like two steaming tea kettles outside Fenwick's fancy, well-maintained townhouse. People moving quickly through the streets gave him odd looks, probably wondering who would be foolish enough to stand out in the cold on a day like today, but offered him small waves or nods.

As he waited, Micah searched outside of Fenwick's house for the plaque that the candy seller had mentioned. It was surprisingly hard to find, and had it not been the dead of winter, he probably would not have found it at all—it would have been covered by high bushes. It was rusted over and barely legible, and an iron facsimile of a sword hung above it.

"In honor of courage most valiant, and honor most high, the town of Roseyard recognizes Douglas Fenwick for his battle with the Beast of the Forest" it read, or at least that was what Micah guessed it said. He curled his lip at it, especially the text below it saying that it was paid for by the townhead—which had been Douglas Fenwick at the time. It seemed in bad taste to award oneself a plaque for something that didn't even need to be done.

After half an hour, Marion strode out of the house, throwing the door open with a bang. Behind her, Fenwick stood with a strange expression on his face. It was half satisfaction, probably because he finally had the land, and half frustration, probably because he had just spent the last half hour on the receiving end of Marion's ire. His eyes caught Micah's and there was a flash of that hunger again.

"Mr. Harlow," he said, a toothy smile spreading on his face. "Have you come to sell your land as well?"

"No such luck, Mr. Fenwick," Marion spat at him. "Mr. Harlow is just a gentleman and refused to let me come into town on my lonesome. He's not selling anything to you."

"I see," Fenwick said, smile refusing to falter. "Well, Mr. Harlow, I do hope that sometime you'll come for tea with me. An open invitation! I have been having the most interesting correspondence with an old friend of yours, a Mr. Edwyn Patterson."

Micah's blood went cold, and it wasn't just the weather. He froze in place, clenching his fists to stop his hand from drifting up to the scars on his throat. Fenwick saw that Micah had stilled like a rabbit about to be devoured by a wolf, and his eyes lit up with predatory glee.

"I believe we have much to discuss," Fenwick said, letting his eyes linger, before he shut the door.

The moment that Fenwick's eyes weren't pinning him in place, Micah's legs threatened to collapse beneath him. He barely caught himself against Wilbur and he couldn't get enough air, even though his breath puffed around him in huge clouds. He squeezed his eyes shut and wrapped his arms around Wilbur's neck, only to see Edwyn's face staring back at him. At first it was the smile, the smile he had seen so many times, but it twisted into something else, the scowl he had on his face when two of his men held Micah down and Edwyn...

"Micah!" He felt a slap on his shoulder from Marion. It seemed likely that she had been trying to get his attention for quite some time.

"Sorry," he said shakily, stroking Wilbur's neck, apologizing as much to him as to Marion.

"Come on, we're going to get you a drink," Marion said, turning on her heel and moving down the street.

"Oh, it's fine, I'm fine," Micah said, shaking his head. "I don't need—"

"It's not. You're not. You do, and I just got a whole lot of money," Marion said, whipping around to face him. "My treat. No arguing."

Micah couldn't do anything but blink and nod. He followed her to the tavern, the same one that Fenwick had taken him to earlier that year. It was warm and bright inside, a fire roaring in the hearth, lanterns hanging throughout the room, giving the place a warm glow. As soon as he entered the room, Micah began to feel better. Marion found a quiet corner, sat him down, and went to order. It was a bit early, but after the visceral reminder of Edwyn, Micah would indulge.

While Marion was away from the table, he spotted another familiar face. Kay was sitting across from a woman he hadn't seen before, who had dark hair intricately braided and woven with gold and whose skin was dark as well. They were speaking quietly and he watched as Kay nodded solemnly and reached to the woman's chest, tugging out an incredibly small writhing black mass. Micah didn't mean to eavesdrop, but he did.

"That's it? That's all there is?" the woman asked, her brow furrowing in confusion.

"Sometimes the sin is holding onto something that isn't your fault," Kay said, opening her mouth and swallowing the mass. "And that is nothing big. I hope you feel lighter, though."

The woman nodded and stood, looking back at Kay one last time before leaving the tavern. It wasn't until the woman was out of sight that Kay let her face twist into the expression of disgust she always had after eating a sin. She drank from the tankard in front of her, then caught Micah staring. Her brow wrinkled in concern, and she got up and joined him at the table.

"Are you all right?" she asked.

"Sorry, I wasn't meaning to be nosey, with you and your client," Micah said with a wince.

"What?" Kay said, brow furrowing. "No, that's...whatever. You look ill. What happened?"

"Fenwick happened," Marion said, returning to the table carrying two large mugs of steaming golden liquid. "And something else."

"Ah," Kay said. "Sorry he's giving you a hard time."

"It's not..." Micah sighed and folded his hands in front of him.

Marion and Kay stared as if trying to will the story out of him. Micah watched as Marion's eyes drifted to his throat, where his scarf had fallen away, revealing the interlaced scars that stood out on his skin. He hated them, he hated himself for trusting someone who would hurt him like that, but he still couldn't bring himself to hate Edwyn. And that was the worst sin of all.

"What happened?" Marion asked, her voice the gentlest it had ever been.

Hot tears threatened to spill from Micah's eyes and he shook his head, saying, "I can't...I can't talk about it. I'm sorry, I wish I could. I can't even tell Ter—"

He cut himself off, remembering where he was. Instead, he reached for the warm cider and gulped it down quickly, hoping that the alcohol and the warmth would blunt the sharp edges of memory that were cutting into him like a blade against his throat. Marion and Kay exchanged worried looks, but they didn't press further. Sometimes he wished someone would, that someone would turn him over and shake it out of him. Maybe then it wouldn't be shackling him down.

When they had said their goodbyes to Kay and were trudging through the snow to his cottage, Marion started whistling. It was a low, sad song that made Micah taste salt water at the back of his throat. The melody reminded him of something his mother would have sung, something he might hum, but bittersweet. He exchanged a glance with Wilbur, who snorted at him. The donkey was the only one here who knew what had happened. Well, Fenwick now probably knew Edwyn's twisted version of the story. Micah couldn't help laughing to himself when he realized that the creature who knew him best in the whole world was a donkey.

When she had finished, Micah took up the task of song master, humming the tune he had hummed on his way to his first market in Roseyard, the one that his mother had sung whenever they had gone to market back in Steephall. The one about safety, protection, and luck. As he finished, Marion chuckled to herself.

"What?" Micah asked, turning from the path to look back at her.

"Nothing," Marion said. "It's just rather funny to me that you cast a lot of spells for someone who insists that he's not a witch."

"Spells?" Micah's brows furrowed in confusion. "I'm not casting any spells. I don't know how."

"And what do you call what you were just doing, young man?" Marion demanded, her eyes twinkling in the gray winter day.

"I was just humming a song my mother used to sing," Micah said. "It's just a song."

"Right," Marion said. "And that's why I felt safe and protected while you were humming, why it looked like you were practically glowing."

"I mean, it's a nice song," Micah said, floundering. "And that's what the lyrics were about, but they were in the old tongue and I don't remember them, just the meaning and the melody."

"What about the song you'd hum when you were taking care of me?" Marion said, looking smug. "What did the words of that song mean?"

Micah was quiet for a moment, contemplating the meaning of this, then said, "For healing, warmth, and comfort."

"And I'll tell you, I felt better much quicker than I expected to," Marion said. "Do you hum those songs when you spin your honey?"

"Yes," Micah said softly.

"You're more of a witch than you think, Mr. Harlow," Marion said, smiling. "And as I said, if there was one thing that Roseyard needed, it was a hedgewitch. And I think you've more than proved that."

Micah still didn't know if he believed her, but he turned the thought over in his head again and again the rest of the trip home. He continued to examine it as winter wore on but never could decide if he completely believed it. Surely, if he were a witch, he would have known. And if he had magic, the events in Steephall wouldn't have happened.

Marion left in the spring. Her daughter and son-in-law arrived with a horse-drawn wagon and packed up all the belongings that had temporarily become part of his small cottage. The daughter, Ellie was her name, apologized profusely to Micah for not coming sooner and thanked him a hundred times over for taking care of Marion.

"Oh, truly, it was no trouble," Micah said. "Marion was taking care of me, half the time."

"He's an insidious liar," Marion said, grinning at him. "He doesn't want to be thanked for a single thing he's done, so he'll pretend he didn't do it."

Ellie laughed and said, "Oh, mother likes you quite a bit, Mr. Harlow. That's an accomplishment."

"Pish!" Marion said, but she wrapped Micah in a bony hug and whispered in his ear, "Don't let Fenwick take what's yours. You be happy now, Mr. Harlow. Keep your magic alive."

He felt oddly empty as he watched them rattle down the road. His neighbor was gone, and a friend too, and now he was much more isolated. So he did what he always did when he felt impossibly lonely. He went into the forest.

He had been experimenting with planting saplings and shrubs at the tree line, trying to expand Terran's reach, if only slightly. Now the tree line was a mere twenty feet from his cottage. It was full of small, scraggly little trees that he had dug out of the ground elsewhere and moved here, but it had worked. Terran was able to introduce himself to the trees and move closer and closer to the cottage. Micah donned the newly repaired straw hat and went to see the one person he knew would never hurt him, who could always make him smile. Terran was already waiting for Micah when he stepped through the trees.

"Hello, my sweet," Terran said, wrapping an arm around Micah's waist and twirling him around. "What would you like from the forest today? Spring is here, everything is waking up and beautiful."

Micah laughed, already feeling better, and said, "I don't need anything, love, but why don't you give me the springtime tour?"

Terran grinned and said, "That I can do."

Terran showed him the new growing buds, the fox kits running through the underbrush, the mud from the melting snow now squirming with worms. Micah smiled at them as Terran swept his arms out, speaking about each little thing. He laughed happily as Terran took his hand and pressed a kiss to it, letting him go. By the time Micah left the forest, he felt lighter, happier, more himself. He almost skipped through the woods, catching the movements of insects and small animals and grinning at them.

Two nights later, everything fell apart.

Micah was sleeping, but he bolted up out of bed the moment he smelled smoke. The house was burning. Out. He needed to get out. He was wearing only a loose tunic and linen pants. No shoes, of course. He panicked and scrambled though his room, then rushed out, grabbing only his hat.

Outside of the bedroom was an inferno. Flames danced madly around the room, licking at him with heat. Black smoke filled the air, and Micah dropped to not breathe it in, already coughing. The fire was shockingly fierce. Had he left the oven on? It couldn't have been the hearth fire, since he remembered collecting the ashes.

As he stumbled around, fumbling for the door, eyes shut against the smoke, he tripped and fell over something round and burning. He opened his watering eyes just a slit. A torch. A *torch*.

All the blood drained from Micah's face. No, no, no. He was liked here, he had friends. He didn't…they couldn't…Coughing, he got to the door and shoved it open just as another lit torch crashed through a window and landed on the floor of his burning home.

Micah broke out into the cool night, sputtering onto the wet, dewy grass on his hands and knees. He took in lungfuls of air, listening to men shout as the house behind him burned. He lifted his head and saw figures by the hen house knocking it with cudgels, smashing it to the ground. He saw a pile of feathers and limp bodies, blood slowly pooling out around it. In one man's hands was a tawny-colored hen, flapping and squawking wildly. Micah was still struggling up from the ground when the man twisted his hands and broke the bird's neck, dropping it to the pile. Micah crashed into him, screaming.

The man hadn't been expecting it, and he was knocked to the ground despite his height and bulk. Micah swung his fists wildly, but the man easily blocked his blows. Micah had worked so hard, *so hard*, to build this place. How dare these people destroy it? Who even were they?

"Get him off me!" the man shouted.

Suddenly, two sets of rough hands yanked Micah off of the hen-killer and dragged him away. He kicked and screamed, even bit them when he could reach their skin. However, the two full-grown men easily overpowered him, sucker punching him when he got a bit too close to breaking free. They dragged him to the back of the cottage, forcing him to his knees.

The garden was ablaze, the odor of burning rosemary and sage overwhelming in the night air. Then he watched yet another man shove a lit torch into the beehive. The hutch erupted in flames as Micah screamed in horror and tried desperately to pull free. He couldn't break away from these strangers' death grip.

"No! No! No!" Micah screamed as he writhed, watching bees exploding out of the hutch, only to be caught in smoke and flame.

Everything…everything was gone again. A sob hitched in his chest and his scars ached. Then someone walked out from the front of the house dragging an extremely unwilling Wilbur and everything clicked into place. The large, imposing figure with a finely cut suit, even during a violent raid in the middle of the night, his slick hair pulled back, and a smile on his face that would wither flowers. Charles Fenwick.

"Mr. Harlow," Fenwick said, his voice a mockery of sympathy. "What a shame! It seems that you were attacked by scoundrels in the middle of the night! What horror, what tragedy! Well, at least you survived, for now."

There was a chorus of deep, dark laughter from all around him. Tears streamed down Micah's soot-covered face. His lungs were scorched, his throat ached. Fenwick handed Wilbur's lead off and stalked over to Micah, then crouched down in front of him and smiled cruelly. He reached out and placed two fingers on Micah's necklace of scars, sending a chill down his spine.

"Your dear old friend was very enlightening," Fenwick said. "Mr. Patterson told me all sorts of things, things that I, at first, struggled to believe. That is, until I visited Mr. Henderson. Magic, Mr. Harlow. I didn't think you were capable of that."

"I never…" Micah couldn't speak properly, only rasp. "I never practiced magic. My mother was a hedgewitch, but not me."

"Oh, but the altars! The prayers to an old god!" Fenwick said. "There's a name for your kind. Not witch, but *warlock*."

Micah shook his head, but it was too much. He was trembling, barely able to keep himself upright. This wasn't happening, couldn't be real.

"What do you want?" Micah croaked.

"The same thing I've been asking for this whole time," Fenwick said. "Your land, Mr. Harlow. I'll even still pay you for it."

That shocked Micah. His head shot up, looking at Fenwick in utter confusion and bewilderment. His land? He would burn a man's house down, destroy his livelihood, murder his animals, for land?

"Why?" Micah asked. "You're the richest man in town, why *my* land?"

"This land belongs to my family. Maybe not on paper, yet, but it is ours. The Fenwicks have been here for generations. It is ours by right," Fenwick said. "We've made progress, but this damn forest is in the way. And I always do things the legal way. I will purchase the land."

Micah looked at him in disbelief and sputtered out, "This is legal?"

"Well, no, but we'll keep this secret between us," Fenwick said, patting Micah's cheek. "After all, don't want the town to know that you're a warlock. This is just…incentive to hurry up the selling process."

"I'm not a warlock."

"Well, Mr. Edwyn Patterson seems to think differently, doesn't he?" Fenwick said, fingers against Micah's scars again.

"Edwyn was…confused," Micah said, and then a realization hit him like a rock. "When Marion's roof fell in…that was you, wasn't it?"

"Mrs. Beath was getting annoyingly stubborn in her old age," Fenwick sighed. "She needed a little incentive too. So, what do you say? Do we have a deal?"

Micah stared coldly at Fenwick and then said, "Fuck you."

Fenwick sighed and stood up, beckoning the man holding Wilbur's lead. "I was really hoping to be polite about this. David, a little more incentive for Mr. Harlow, if you would."

Fenwick took several steps back as Wilbur was pulled in front of Micah. Another man came up behind the donkey, who was looking at Micah with desperate eyes. Knowing what was coming, Micah fought wildly against the men holding him and got kicked and punched and pushed into the ground for his trouble. The whole time he was screaming, begging 'no' over and over again, but a knife was brought up to Wilbur's throat, and the man slit it with ease.

Blood sprayed over the grass, and over Micah, as Wilbur shrieked and Micah screamed. Micah went limp in the men's arms, sobbing into the earth. Wilbur had been the most steadfast thing in his life for the longest time…he was his mother's donkey before Micah was even born. Micah was screaming, words that didn't even make sense, and he was done. He wanted to die. Everything was gone now.

Fenwick stepped breezily over the donkey's corpse to Micah and plucked his mother's straw hat off his head. It was a miracle it had stayed on. He threw it to the flames where it quickly burned to nothing. Micah didn't even care. The men let go of his arms, leaving him lying on the grass, staring into Wilbur's dead eyes.

"Oh, now, come," Fenwick said. "It was just a donkey, Mr. Harlow."

Micah didn't say anything. He just lay there, listening to the world burn around him. He thought maybe he heard someone screaming his name, but it sounded far away.

"What was that?" one of the men asked.

"Nothing, probably a night bird," Fenwick said with a wave of his hand. "Anyway, Mr. Harlow, offer still stands. I'll buy your land. Move you on to a new town, perhaps. Or maybe I'll keep you here. Mr. Patterson did mention you had other talents."

Fenwick reached out a foot and turned Micah onto his back. Micah had been lying as though he were already dead, but at that insinuation he went red, his face covered in burning shame. Why would Edwyn tell Fenwick about *that* of all things? Again, he heard his name. It was closer now.

"You had to have heard that," the same man said.

"What do you say, Mr. Harlow?" Fenwick continued, ignoring the man. "I'll give you a good fair price."

"Why don't you just kill me?" Micah managed, a sob breaking the sentence in half.

"Bad optics," Fenwick said with a shrug. "I don't like to get my hands dirty. Unfortunately, you made some friends in town."

Micah laughed at that, but it turned into a sob in his throat. He lowered his hands and looked up at Fenwick, who was once again twisting the brass ring on his finger. The promise to Marion echoed in his mind. Micah just shook his head.

"Stubborn," Fenwick said with a sigh. "Loosen him up."

The men started kicking him. Micah curled in on himself, covering his face, hugging his legs to his belly. If he survived this, he would be bruised all the way to hell and back again. Eventually, they stopped. His name was being called again. This time there was no mistaking it, and it was close. It was coming from the trees.

"It was his fucking name!" the man from before said, pointing at Micah's crumpled form. "You heard that!"

"Who is that, Mr. Harlow?" Fenwick asked from his position about fifteen feet away. Probably too far away.

As they looked to Micah for an answer, he summoned what strength he had left and rolled over towards the woods. He picked himself up as he did so, stumbling and running towards the tree line. It was so close.

"Well, get him! Fools!" Fenwick shouted at the stunned men.

They gave chase and far too quickly one of them caught up. He grabbed Micah around the waist and slammed him into a tree. A *tree*. The fire from the still-burning house lit the two of them eerily. The man's snarling face turned into one of confusion as he looked at Micah.

"Why are you smiling?" he asked.

Micah didn't get a chance to answer because the man was torn off of him and thrown out of the forest. He landed with a sickening snap and a scream, breaking at least one limb. Micah fell to the ground and looked up, seeing Terran as he had never seen him before. His chest was heaving, his fingers had extended into claws, his lips were pulled back in a snarl that revealed sharp teeth. Even the antlers, always so beautiful, had turned sharp and deadly. Terran growled at the men closing in on Micah.

"What is *that*?" one man shouted, stopping in his tracks.

"It's the beast! The beast of the forest!" another screamed.

Terran charged at them then, throwing them as he had the other man, out of the forest in huge arcs. There were more snaps and screams. Micah pulled himself up and walked unsteadily to Terran as he stood at the tree line snarling at the men. He gently placed a hand on Terran's arm.

Terran's head snapped around to Micah, but as soon as he saw who it was, he softened, shifting back to the form Micah knew. Micah was swaying on his feet, struggling to stay upright. As he collapsed, Terran caught him and gently scooped him up.

"What have they done to you, my sweet?" Terran murmured in his ear as he turned and carried him into the forest.

Micah looked over Terran's shoulder, seeing Fenwick glaring at the two of them while the men Terran had tossed picked themselves up slowly. His lip was curled in a snarl and somehow his wolf eyes connected with Micah's in the dark. It was the last thing Micah saw before darkness took him.

7

———

THE DARK

IN THE DARKNESS OF SLEEP, MICAH DREAMED. NO, remembered. Remembered in near perfect accuracy what had happened in Steephall. The thing that Micah could not face, let alone speak about.

Micah's mother had died when he was seventeen. It had devastated him. She had gotten sick in a way that neither her magic nor his care could fix. She suffered for a year and then she died. He buried her himself. He closed himself off from the world for years, only caring for the bees and Wilbur the donkey. Not wanting the bees or the donkey to die had probably saved his life. Who would take care of them if he died? As the years went on, he started living for himself as well.

Five years later, he was known as a hermit. Perhaps rumored to be a hedgewitch, if people were being generous. He lived a mile outside of town, and people journeyed to him with their sore throats or colds. They asked him for advice on their gardens, and he gave it, helping where he could, but not venturing into town outside of market days. He couldn't be with that many people at once, preferring the solitude of the forest.

He first met Edwyn Patterson on one of those market days. He had his boards set up, jars of honey, cookies, soap, and candles all laid out on a faded blue cloth that just touched the ground. He was far too quiet in those days to ask for a better spot, so without his mother to protest, he always ended up on the outskirts of the market.

A young man with a panicked look in his eye ran down the street, spotted Micah's very unbusy booth, and sprinted over. Anyone with eyes could see that the man was extremely beautiful. He had creamy olive skin, unblemished by any mark, deep, gray-blue eyes that sparkled in the sun, and wavy, ink-black hair that fell to his shoulders. He was like a fox, springing and agile and a wonder to watch. As he bolted towards Micah, he sat up in a panic.

"Uh," Micah managed to say, very articulate he was back then.

"Hide me, please," the young man said, ducking under the table and disappearing. "Don't tell them I'm here!"

Moments later, a squad of four burly-looking young men, red-faced with anger, came stomping down the street. Micah understood their rage: blue ink dripped into the dirt of the street from splotches all over their shirts. One of them pointed suddenly at Micah.

"You haven't seen Edwyn Patterson around here, have you?" he yelled.

"Uh, who?" Micah said, flinching.

"Ah, shit, you're the freak from the woods," the ink-stained man groaned. "Little rich shit, black hair, blue eyes, looks just *so innocent*."

Micah fought the urge to look under his table at the beautiful young man whom this angry knot of a person had just described so accurately, if unkindly. Instead, Micah just shrugged.

"Not here," another man groaned. "Come on, let's keep looking. Maybe we'll get a good punch or two in before his father arrives."

They left, and Micah waited a full two minutes before leaning under the table and whispering, "They're gone."

Edwyn popped out, rearranged his hair, and grinned a fantastic grin before saying, "Ah, you're a blessing. Thank you. Edwyn Patterson, though I'm sure you figured that out."

He offered a hand to Micah, who took it with only a bit of hesitation as he said, "Micah Harlow. And, uh, it was no trouble."

"Could have been, Micah Harlow, could have been!" Edwyn said, still smiling. "But for your quick thinking!"

"If a shrug is quick thinking," Micah said, feeling his face grow hot at the string of compliments from such a handsome young man.

"Nonetheless, saved me from a bit of unpleasantness," Edwyn said with a wink. "Come by my place sometime. Biggest one in town, can't miss it. Oh, suppose I should buy something, for your troubles."

Edwyn picked up a jar of honey and then flicked Micah a gold coin, easily ten times its value, without even asking the price. Micah caught the coin and watched in stunned silence as Edwyn threw another wink his way and disappeared down an alley.

That was the start of it.

Edwyn began to visit Micah's booth on market days, talking with him about all kinds of things. Micah learned much about the inner workings of the Patterson household, the grievances that Edwyn had against his father because he forbade him to continue at university in the large city of Silverchill, his annoyance that his mother kept trying to push him together with the Frostworth girl ("I mean, have you seen her teeth?"), and the constant pranks that he found endlessly amusing but that his father was getting sick of. Edwyn was three years Micah's senior, but Micah felt as though he were the older, wiser one in the conversations as he doled out advice when it was asked of him.

"You see, that's why I like you, Micah Harlow." Edwyn said with a grin. "You always know the right thing to say."

Micah always ended up blushing when he said things like that. And because he always called him "Micah Harlow", his full name. He said it rolled off the tongue beautifully, unlike his own name. Micah had insisted, of course, that "Edwyn Patterson" also sounded nice, but Edwyn wouldn't hear of it.

The only thing that Edwyn didn't seem to like about Micah was that he sometimes gave things away, like his mother always had. A young mother at her wits' end with her three little ones, well, four cookies wouldn't be missed. Someone with a sore throat and no way to pay, a bit of the honey candy would go a long way and it cost him very little. Once, even, when a young woman with dirty, tangled hair desperately wanted to go to the dance, a cake of soap was worth the loss to see her smile.

"I don't understand why you do that," Edwyn said once, shaking his head. "Your products are too good to give away for free."

"It's just a bit of kindness," Micah said, shrugging. "I think it'll come around threefold someday for me."

"Are you suggesting that all my pranks will catch up with me, Micah Harlow?" Edwyn said, his signature grin on his face.

"Oh, no!" Micah said, holding up his hands. "I didn't mean to insinuate…I just…my apologies, Mr. Patterson."

Edwyn snorted with laughter and said, "You're so easy to fluster, Micah Harlow. It's cute."

Micah turned the sound of Edwyn's voice saying "cute" over and over for about three months. He only stopped because Edwyn came to visit him. Micah had been taking care of the bees when he heard the telltale crunch of feet on the trail leading to the Harlow cottage—he still didn't think of it as his own, even five years after her death.

"Just a moment! I'll be with you shortly!" Micah called as he finished with the apiary.

When he got to the front of the house and saw Edwyn, he froze. The handsome young man looked out of place. This was Micah's small, little cottage, full of bees and herbs and donkey-smell. Edwyn was far too rich and elegant to be *here*. He belonged in town, not the woods. When Edwyn saw Micah, however, he lit up.

"Micah Harlow! I was told I'd find you here and I hardly believed it!" Edwyn said, grinning and walking forward.

"Hello, Mr. Patterson," Micah said, still in shock.

Edwyn snorted and patted Micah on the shoulder. "Edwyn, please. No one from town is here, so let's not bother with the formalities. What's with the ridiculous hat?"

Edwyn flicked the brim of the straw hat on Micah's head, the one that had been his mother's. Gripping it so it wouldn't fall off, Micah blushed.

"It was my mother's, she left it for me," he said quietly. "It keeps the sun off my face when I'm working outside."

"You're already freckled to hell and back," Edwyn said. "Why bother? Anyway, come on. Show me your quaint little home."

Micah blushed furiously but led Edwyn inside. He hung the hat on a rack, reluctant to see Edwyn's expression when he saw the little kitchen with dried herbs hanging and old, battered furniture. He sighed and turned, only to see Edwyn looking at him with curiosity.

"You live here?" he asked, with maybe a trace of superiority, but no malice.

"Yes," Micah said, eyes dropping to the ground.

"Huh," Edwyn said. "I guess that makes sense. What with you being a witch, and all."

"Oh, I'm not a witch."

"Sure," Edwyn said, rolling his eyes and running his fingers across a battered old chair's time-smoothed wood. "You like living out here, all by yourself?"

"Well," Micah said, rubbing the back of his neck, ashamed for no reason. "We couldn't really have the bees in town, they scare folks, and I don't mind it. I'm not very good with…people."

Edwyn huffed a small laugh and said, "You certainly won me over."

"You're an exception. I've never been very good at it," Micah said. "Talking, that is."

Edwyn moved closer and placed a thumb on Micah's mouth, rubbing carefully across the bottom lip. Micah, stunned, stood awed and motionless.

Edwyn smiled and said, "There's a lot of people in town that would be dying for a chance like this. Don't waste it."

Micah didn't exactly know what Edwyn meant until he removed his thumb and pressed his lips to Micah's. Micah stumbled a bit in surprise. *Don't waste it.* Well, he wasn't going to.

A few hours later, Micah was laying in the bed, still bewildered and breathing hard, and watching as Edwyn re-dressed, doing up his buttons and smiling lazily. Micah swallowed, watching the soft, unblemished skin disappear beneath clothes that cost more than he made in a year.

"That wasn't bad," Edwyn said. "First time?"

Micah nodded, unsure how this had even happened. He blinked, dazed. Edwyn smirked at him.

"Next time, I'll give you a heads up so you can bathe," Edwyn said. "You smelled a bit like a donkey, no offense."

"Sorry," Micah said softly.

Edwyn shrugged and said, "You'll know for next time. See you."

After Micah heard the front door close, he lay in bed staring up at the ceiling for what felt like hours before he got up, washed, and continued with his chores. He kept touching his bottom lip where Edwyn had run his thumb. When he was brushing down Wilbur for the night, he couldn't help but laugh.

"He doesn't like the way you smell, but I don't mind it," Micah said to Wilbur, who shook his head and snorted.

EDWYN'S VISITS WERE SPORADIC; SOMETIMES ON A MARKET DAY, Edwyn would saunter up to tell Micah he'd be visiting him the next day. That night, Micah would scrub his skin until it was raw and do so again the next morning. After all that, Edwyn would only show up about half the time. Other times, a visitor to the cottage would slip Micah a note from Mr. Patterson, usually reading some variation of "see you tomorrow." Edwyn kept his appointments made that way with more consistency. Micah's world spun on the axis of Edwyn Patterson's flights of fancy.

It lasted a long time, and while he enjoyed Edwyn, he somehow felt his mother wouldn't have liked the man. Something deep in his gut told him this, or maybe the way that Wilbur flicked his ears back, or the fact that Edwyn was the only person that Wilbur had ever bitten. But Edwyn was unlike anyone Micah had ever known, and he just couldn't stop.

One day in the fourth year of their strange relationship, Edwyn came completely unannounced. It wasn't ever a constant thing; once Edwyn had left for nine months without a word to Micah, only for a note to appear at his door one random day telling him to be ready tomorrow. But since that first day, he had always told Micah when he was coming. This time, he just showed up.

Micah was working in the garden, his shirt and arms covered in dirt and his mother's straw hat shading his face. He was humming to himself, not aware of his surroundings at all, when the hat was plucked from his head without warning. He jumped, stumbled back, fell on his rear, and looked up to see Edwyn twirling the hat on one finger.

"I can't believe you're still wearing this old thing, Micah Harlow," he said, smirking down at Micah.

"It's practical," Micah murmured, then swallowed and said, "I didn't know you were coming, sorry. I must have missed the note. I'm not cleaned up at all, but if you don't mind waiting I can—"

"I'm not here for that," Edwyn said, laughing and hanging the hat on a fence post. "I need your other services."

"Oh!" Micah was surprised. Edwyn had never asked for anything but his body before. Micah pulled himself up out of the garden and brushed the dirt off of his shirt and hands.

"Can you make a sleeping draught?" Edwyn asked, and there was a bit of desperation in his voice that concerned Micah deeply.

"Probably," Micah said. "Are you having trouble sleeping?"

Edwyn snorted, crossed his arms, and with a distant look in his eyes said, "Yeah, you could say that."

"I can do that, I know my mother had a recipe. I'm not that naturally good at brewing, but I can follow a recipe," Micah said.

"Ah, so you *are* a hedgewitch," Edwyn said, his signature smirk returning.

"I don't think I should besmirch the good name of hedgewitches everywhere by claiming that," Micah said, moving towards the cottage. "But a witch's son who knows a few tricks, sure."

He brought Edwyn into the kitchen and got to work. He scrubbed the dirt from his arms, hands, and face after Edwyn made a remark about it, then changed his shirt. Edwyn watched him carefully as he did this, then started cackling as Micah donned an apron and tied the strings.

"What?" Micah asked as he pulled his mother's recipe book down from its nook.

"Nothing," Edwyn said, leaning against a counter with a disdainful smile. "You just look like a housewife."

Micah frowned and resisted asking why, exactly, that was something to laugh at. Sometimes Edwyn befuddled him. But the memory of the note of desperation in Edwyn's voice and the worried expression on his face compelled Micah to keep working. He flipped to the sleeping draught recipe and read it over carefully, twice. Then he started gathering ingredients.

He ground dried lavender and peppermint in a mortar and pestle, adding almond skins as the herbs were crushed to a fine powder. He scraped the dry ingredients into a simmering pot of water. Of course, he swirled in teaspoons of honey. The final ingredient he checked six times over before adding three small drops of belladonna to the mixture with shaking hands. After a minute, he pulled the boiling concoction off the heat and covered it.

"It'll have to sit and steep for an hour. I'm sorry," Micah said.

"Well, if that's what it says," Edwyn sighed, and leaned his head back against a cupboard.

"I do want to tell you about this sleeping draught, this is very important," Micah said, staring into Edwyn's eyes. "For someone your size, you should only take three drops. If you take more, you might never wake up. It's very potent. There's nightshade in it. Only three drops, and I'd put it in tea or something, not take it directly."

Edwyn nodded, then looked out the window, "What if it were for someone bigger than me? How many drops then?"

Micah's stomach twisted and he said, "This is for you, isn't it, Edwyn? You're not going to give this to anyone without…without their consent, right?"

Edwyn's head snapped back to Micah, a look of anger lingering briefly on his face before it shifted back into his lazy, easy smile, and he said, "Of course. Just curious."

There was a voice in the back of Micah's head, then, like a needle stabbing into him over and over. *Don't give it to him. You can't trust him. Stop.* But that voice faded away when Edwyn stepped close and smiled.

"An hour, huh?" Edwyn asked, moving his thumb up to Micah's lower lip. "I wonder what we can do to keep ourselves entertained? How closely do you need to watch that?"

"It doesn't need my full attention," Micah said.

An hour later, Micah's knees and throat were sore and he was pouring the finished draught into a bottle for Edwyn, who was leaning against the doorframe watching him carefully. As Micah stoppered the bottle, that voice was back in his head, begging him not to give it to Edwyn, that it wasn't too late, but he ignored it.

"Remember, just three drops," Micah said, placing the bottle in Edwyn's hands.

"Just three," Edwyn repeated.

Micah smiled and, feeling a bit daring, leaned in to kiss Edwyn, but Edwyn pushed him back and murmured something about being late. Micah stood in the doorway, watching him leave, an empty feeling in the pit of his stomach.

Only two months later, Edwyn was back for more of the draught. Micah was shocked that he had gotten through it that fast, and worried that he was over-dosing himself. *Or,* the traitor voice at the back of his mind said, *it's not for him at all.* But he shook that thought away and agreed to make another batch. Micah was out of nightshade berries, so he needed to go into the forest to gather them. He promised the disgruntled Edwyn that he would be quick. As Micah was grabbing bread and cheese and milk, Edwyn sneered at him.

"Why are you packing lunch? I thought you were going to be quick," he said.

"Oh, this is just the offering," Micah said. "For the forest spirit."

"You still do that?" Edwyn said, disdain in his voice.

"Of course," Micah said, a little distressed that Edwyn was so sour towards an offering. "Everyone who forages does. It's tradition. Keeping the old ways."

"Civilized men do not need to keep 'the old ways,'" Edwyn said with a smirk. "Leave it here, take what you need. I'm sure it will be fine."

Micah usually just gave in to Edwyn's opinions, but not about this. This was fundamental, something that his mother had instilled in him since he got big enough to toddle behind her through the trees. Micah set his face and looked Edwyn square in the eyes.

"I suppose I am not civilized then. I'm keeping the old ways," Micah said, and the firmness of his voice seemed to take Edwyn by surprise. "I'll be back soon."

His heart was pounding as he turned and marched towards the woods. It was so loud in his ears that he didn't even hear Edwyn behind him until he was almost to the altar. He turned back, blinking in surprise when he saw him.

"I didn't realize it was so important to you," Edwyn said, and that was probably as close to an apology as Micah was going to get from him.

"Sorry, I didn't mean to get angry," Micah said, shaking his head and continuing to the altar.

"It's fine," Edwyn said with another smirk. "I'll be civilized enough for the both of us."

That sat ill with Micah, too, but he chose to ignore it. He went through his ceremonies, then gathered what he needed and headed back, Edwyn at his heels the entire time, a bemused look on his face. Micah made the draught and gave it, hesitantly, to Edwyn, despite his half-formed suspicion that something was wrong.

SOMETHING *WAS* WRONG, EXTREMELY WRONG, BECAUSE AT THE next market, Edwyn's father, Dorin Patterson, came storming down the rows. When he spotted Micah, he charged towards him. The prey instinct to flee had Micah scrambling up out of his seat, but freezing won out in the end.

Patterson grabbed Micah by the front of his shirt and yanked him into the cobblestoned street. Those tending the booths near him averted their eyes, their customers scurrying away. If Edwyn Patterson was a fox, Dorin Patterson was a bear. He gripped Micah's shoulder with one massive hand and twisted the front of his shirt in the other. Micah was shaking and only barely managed not to start crying.

"What is my son doing visiting you out in the woods?" Patterson said in a low growl.

Micah panicked. He didn't know what would be worse for Edwyn: revealing that he and Edwyn had been sleeping together or that Edwyn was coming to him for a sleeping draught. He was hovering in the air, his toes barely scraping against the ground, trying to start a sentence and failing over and over, when he spotted a lithe-moving Edwyn over his father's shoulder.

"Oh, let go of the poor man, father," Edwyn said. "It was a tryst, that's all."

Patterson dropped Micah unceremoniously to the ground. Micah tried to land on his feet, he truly did, but he slipped and fell to his back, the air knocked out of him. He was pulling himself up to a sitting position when Patterson loomed over him.

"Never speak to my son again, do you understand?"

Micah nodded. As Edwyn gave him an apologetic look from behind his father, Patterson stalked over to Micah's board. He took hold of the table and flipped it, sending soaps and candles flying, cracking on the ground. Cookies scattered through the dirt and jars of honey shattered, covering the ground with golden stickiness. The townsfolk at the booths next to his flinched, and one woman even yelped, but no one would look Dorin Patterson, the richest man in town, in the eye.

Micah was really fighting tears now. A full month of work destroyed. Dorin Patterson stalked towards the center of town, leaving Micah sitting on the ground looking at the remnants of his wares. A shadow fell above him and he saw Edwyn. He smiled, not his usual cocky smirk but something much softer, and held something out to him. Micah tried to force himself to move, but he couldn't. After a moment, Edwyn dropped ten gold coins to the ground with a clatter.

"He's really just mad that I've been sneaking out at all," Edwyn said quietly. "He just gets so tired at night these days, and he doesn't hear me leave to go out with friends. He says I need to be more responsible."

Edwyn scoffed and laughed, waiting for Micah's response. When it was clear that Micah wasn't going to say anything, Edwyn continued, "People have seen me go into the forest, servants and the like. I had to admit to something, but that should pay for what he destroyed. I'm sure it'll be forgotten soon, Micah Harlow. He is just so sleepy these days."

Then he left.

Micah eventually picked himself up, and then his destroyed wares. He loaded up the cart and walked slowly back to his cottage. The townsfolk did nothing, just watched him, averting their eyes any time he looked back at them. He had never felt so utterly and completely alone., even when his mother had just died.

FOR THE NEXT THREE MONTHS, HE DIDN'T LEAVE HIS LAND. HE survived off of what he could forage, took care of the bees and Wilbur, and was alone. People stopped coming to the cottage. He became more dependent on the forest, always leaving offerings so his bounty was usually quite good, but he missed the small comforts he could get in town. Cheese and milk, chicken eggs and meat, the sounds of other people, but he dared not risk seeing Edwyn again. Then, of course, Edwyn showed up on his doorstep.

"Micah Harlow," Edwyn said cheerfully, as if nothing had happened. "I need another refill."

"I'm not supposed to talk to you," Micah said, eyes locked on the ground, unable to look at Edwyn's face.

"Oh, pish posh," Edwyn said as he pushed in and set the once-again empty bottle on the counter. "That was months ago. Father was just in one of his moods. The coin I gave you should have paid for what was lost. I've been looking for you at the market. Why aren't you going?"

Micah was staring at him, aghast, unable to believe that someone could be so clueless. He just shook his head and pulled down his mother's book. The voice inside him telling him that this would only mean trouble was now buried so deep that he couldn't even hear it any more. He was gathering the ingredients, starting on the brew, when Edwyn grabbed his wrist and stopped him.

"Are you mad at me, Micah Harlow?" he asked.

Micah stilled, then quietly said, "No."

"Then why are you acting like this?"

"Acting like what?"

"Oh, I don't know, put out or something! You're acting like a child giving a playmate the silent treatment, only I don't know what I did. I stood up for you to my father, you know. He called you a…"

Edwyn wasn't one to trail off, but he did when he saw Micah's tired stare. He stopped speaking and tried one of his easy, lazy smiles, but Micah didn't react the way he always had.

"What did he call me?" Micah asked, his mouth dry.

"A warlock," Edwyn said, then, lifting his hands defensively, added, "I told him that you weren't! I just said that we were having some… fun. You know."

Micah rubbed the bridge of his nose and said, "This is the last time that I will make this for you."

"Oh, come now, why?" Edwyn said, leaning towards Micah, starting to lift his hand to Micah's face, but Micah turned away from him.

"Too much of it can be bad," Micah said. "It can hurt you."

"As you said before," Edwyn murmured as he leaned back against the counter. "I'm not really that worried about it."

"Edwyn, this is for you, isn't it?" Micah asked, turning to face him. "Three drops, just to help you sleep?"

Edwyn stared at him, letting the question hang like smoke between them, until he finally said, "Yes. It's for me. It's the only way I can get through the night."

Micah could tell that it wasn't the whole truth, that there was something else there. But it escaped him, and he didn't want to push any further. He was so tired. He turned back to working on the brew.

Suddenly, Edwyn pushed his way into Micah's view, grinned and tilted his head. "How about, while it's steeping, we have some fun? Old times' sake."

Micah froze in the middle of adding lavender to his mortar and said softly, "I probably smell like a donkey."

"That's what soap and water are for, silly," Edwyn said, tucking a stray lock of inky hair behind his ear and lifting his eyebrows.

"I don't think I want to," Micah said, continuing to work on the brew.

"You don't think?" Edwyn said, and then he sighed and threw up his hands. "Fine, all right. We'll just stare at each other while it finishes."

Micah bit back the desire to give in and finished brewing the draught. While they were waiting for it to finish steeping, Micah made tea and offered a cup to Edwyn, who took a sip and grimaced.

"It's so weak," he said.

"I'm trying to make the leaves last, sorry," Micah said, wincing. "Do you want some honey? Maybe sugar? Though I don't have a lot of that."

"Just come into town and buy some, you're not banned or anything," Edwyn said. "Despite what he thinks, my father actually isn't the authority in town."

Micah shrugged and didn't say anything. Edwyn's tea sat on the table and grew cold. The hour passed and Micah filled the bottle, handing it gingerly to Edwyn. He nodded to Micah and left his cottage.

A week after that, everything fell apart.

IT WAS PAST MIDNIGHT WHEN THEY BROKE DOWN HIS DOOR. Micah sat up in bed blinking his eyes, trying to figure out what was happening. Two men stalked into the cottage and spotted him. Not fully awake, Micah could not understand what was happening at first when they pulled him bodily out of bed and dragged him out of the house.

"What? What's going on?" Micah asked, still trying to wake up.

One of the men jostled him and threw him into the wagon that was parked outside of the cottage. The cool late autumn air snapped him out of drowsiness, but what truly woke him was the vision outside. Men with axes by the hives. His mother's hives.

"What are they doing?" Micah said, his voice shaking.

"Quiet," one of the men who had brought him out snapped and then, to the man at the front of the wagon, "Drive on."

Micah saw the first man pull back to swing on the hive. He was covered from head to toe with quilted fabric, his face covered with mesh. They knew what they were doing. They *knew*. Micah started scrambling out of the moving carriage, but the two men pulled him back. The darkness of the night and the twisting forest road spared him the sight of the hives being destroyed, but the buzzing, furious and frightened, lived in his mind.

"Why? What is happening?" Micah asked after a few punches to the gut and the head had finally stopped his escape attempts.

"Dorin Patterson is dead," one of the men said. "And his son said that you did it. With magic."

"Edwyn?" Micah was stunned for the rest of the ride.

The town square of Steephall looked like it was on fire, but it wasn't. Not really. There were crowds of people swarming around, holding torches. It looked like a funeral pyre in the center of the town, and Edwyn was standing there, arms crossed, his face set.

Micah was hauled out of the wagon and shoved into the center of the square. He was wearing his sleep clothes and didn't even have shoes on. Small rocks that had lodged themselves between the cobblestones dug sharply into the soles of his feet. Heat radiated off of the torches, but the cold night air still bit at him. Edwyn was staring at him in disgust.

"He was right, it seems," Edwyn said, his voice sharp as a tooth.

"Edwyn, what's going on?" Micah asked, wrapping his arms around his middle and shrinking down.

"Oh, you're pretending you don't know!" Edwyn said, laughing humorlessly. "That's rich! That's fantastic! Care to explain this?"

Edwyn pulled the bottle of the sleeping draught out of his bag and threw it at Micah's feet. It hit the ground and shattered into a million pieces, bits of glass burrowing into his shins and the tops of his feet. He yelped and stepped back, a mistake because pieces of glass that had fallen behind him dug into his soles.

"The sleeping draught?" Micah asked, and then he noticed that the bottle had been empty and his blood went cold. "I just made that for you a week ago, where did it all go?"

"You see! He admits it!" Edwyn declared, thrusting a hand at Micah.

The crowd shifted uneasily and stared at Micah. He couldn't help but shuffle his feet, despite the glass digging into his soles, his mind just barely catching up to what was happening. He knew his face must be a mixture of shock and horror, of confusion and pain.

"You were only ever supposed to use three drops at once!" Micah shouted. "And it was only supposed to be for you! Why would you give it to your father?"

"I never meant to," Edwyn said. "I was never to speak to you again, remember? You compelled me to. You used magic to make me kill my father, *warlock*."

"What? I'm not...I can't..." Micah was hardly forming sentences but managed, "Why would I want to kill your father?"

A voice spoke up, then, from the side. She was a woman that Micah knew, someone who had sold vegetables next to him for years. She looked at him with horror and disgust.

"We all saw it," the woman said. "When he pulled you out to yell at you, to get you to stop compelling his son. Then he broke all your wares. We haven't seen you since."

"A clear motive," another man said.

Micah looked up at Edwyn, tears forming in his eyes, and said, "You said I compelled you?"

Guilt flashed momentarily in Edwyn's eyes, but it was quickly banished as he said, "Part of your magic. And there is only one way to stay a warlock's power—besides death, of course."

Micah's arms were grabbed and he was dragged through the broken glass and forced to his knees at Edwyn's feet. Edwyn looked down at him with an unreadable expression. Micah was sure that his own expression was very readable, one of desperation and a misplaced hope that there was something between them, something that would stay his hand. Then Edwyn pulled out an iron dagger.

"Edwyn, please." Tears streamed down Micah's face.

"Warlocks get their powers from demons and old gods, by making deals with them," Edwyn said, twisting the dagger in the air. "You even showed me how you did it, in the woods. So, simply, to stop a warlock, we'll take away his voice."

"Cut out his tongue!" a voice cried from the side, and Micah's eyes went wide in panic.

"Oh, nothing so vulgar as that," Edwyn said, and then as he crouched down, he spoke quietly enough that only Micah could hear, "Besides, I wouldn't want to lose what that tongue can do."

Micah, to his own horror, flushed horribly. What was Edwyn's plan? He tried to break away again, but Edwyn held the knife to his throat. Micah froze. But Edwyn didn't.

None of the cuts were deep enough to cause death, but the problem was that despite his time at university, where he claimed to have studied anatomy, Edwyn didn't know where the vocal cords were. So he kept digging into Micah's throat with the blade. The pain was greater than anything Micah had ever experienced. He pulled back at first, scrambling away from the knife and Edwyn, but that only made it worse. The men holding his arms dug their fingers into his flesh, and his movement caused Edwyn to miss. Small cuts bloomed not only on his throat, but around it as well, until Micah finally gave in. His throat burned and ached, blood flowed, and he started to feel cold and sick.

As the cuts went on, even the most bloodthirsty onlookers started to get uncomfortable as Micah choked, and coughed, and cried. All he could smell was blood, and the world had blurred around him except for the sharp slashes of metal against his throat. The arms holding him had let go as he knelt in front of Edwyn, blood and tears mixing in a puddle on the ground.

Finally, Micah lifted his hand and covered his throat. The knife clattered to the ground and Edwyn took Micah by the shoulders and dragged him up so that he was looking Edwyn in the eyes through the tangled mess of his blond curls. All he could think, looking at the beautiful face framed with black silk hair, was why was Edwyn crying?

"I gave him too much," Edwyn whispered. "He didn't wake up. I was just trying to have a bit of fun. I didn't want to hurt him. I had to tell them something."

Micah didn't say anything. He couldn't if he wanted to; he was holding his throat together. Instead, he simply turned, limped through the broken glass, and walked out of town. The second he stepped into the forest, he was back at his cottage. He blinked, not knowing what had happened, until he glimpsed a figure disappearing behind a tree, one with pointed ears and bark-like skin.

He stumbled to the cottage. The hives were hacked apart, gone. The gardens were burned. When he went inside, his mother's recipe book was torn apart, but other than that, things were largely undamaged.

He treated his wounds the best he could, wrapping his throat, swallowing down healing honey, picking out shards of glass, grunting through the pain. Dawn was just breaking when he was done. Then he started packing. Wilbur and the cart were still undamaged, and that was good. He was leaving Steephall, that was certain.

When he first got to Wilbur, his face twisted and he collapsed against his steady, strong body. Micah's sobs were silent and painful in his throbbing throat. Once he was done weeping, he worked and he worked and he worked. By the time he was finished loading his belongings, the sun was high in the sky.

He limped as he led Wilbur to the road, leaving half the things in the cottage, but still probably taking far too much. As he stumbled out, he spotted a figure in the road. A young man with ink-black hair and an apologetic smile. Edwyn licked his lips and closed the distance between them as Micah reached the road.

"Where are you going?" Edwyn asked, grabbing Micah's arm.

Micah said nothing. He just firmly tugged his arm free from Edwyn's grasp.

"Oh, come now, don't be like that," Edwyn said. "I had to. You understand."

Micah had told himself that he wasn't even going to look at

Edwyn, but at that he had to, staring in shock and disbelief. He blinked and turned away.

Wilbur flicked his tail at Edwyn in disdain.

"You're being ridiculous," Edwyn called. "I didn't cut you that deep. You're alive! This doesn't have to change anything for us."

Micah couldn't even honor that with a look. He just walked on into the uncertain future.

8

THE TOWN

MICAH'S EYES FLUTTERED OPEN. HE COULDN'T REMEMBER WHERE he was or what had happened. Something cool was being pressed to his tender skin. He was lying on his back on something soft and squishy, light from above dappling down on his face through the branches. He breathed in sharply as the cool, wet cloth brushed over a burn. The person moving it froze.

"Micah?" Terran's voice was a familiar low rumble, comforting and sturdy.

At the sound of his name, everything that had happened with Fenwick and the fire and Wilbur came crashing down and Micah could only sob in response. Hot tears ran down his face, and his throat hitched painfully as Terran gently, so gently picked him up and held him. He didn't try to quiet him, just held him while he fell apart, and the only thing he whispered was, "You're safe now, nothing else will hurt you."

Terran was too gentle. Micah wanted him to squeeze him, to make the burns and bruises ache as he deserved. He had let this happen, and everything was destroyed, ruined, because of him. Why was he so stupid? He was always so stupid. His sobs started to subside and Terran carefully set him back down. Micah sat on the soft moss bed

101

under the yew tree, his knees pulled up to his chest, his shoulders still shaking.

"He'll pay for what he's done," Terran said softly, brushing back Micah's hair. "I'm sorry I didn't get there sooner."

"It's my fault," Micah said, his voice cracked and weak. "You don't need to be sorry."

Terran took Micah's shoulders and said, "No, 'tis not your fault, my sweet. Micah, this was not your fault."

Micah scrubbed his eyes with his fists and said, "It was. It always is. And the hive you gave me was destroyed, the hens are all dead, the house is gone, and Wilbur—"

His voice broke then. Fenwick's taunting voice saying that Wilbur was 'just a donkey' echoed in his mind. Then Edwyn's voice rose up, saying that he smelled like a donkey. He was on the edge of sobs again. He couldn't keep doing this, or he would have nothing left. Terran pushed an earthenware bowl full of clear, cool water into his hands. He drank thankfully.

Terran looked at him, his wild green eyes searching Micah's face carefully as he said, "The trees whispered to me, and they told me what happened before. In Steephall. You were dreaming of it under the yew."

Micah lowered the bowl and stared at it, unable to look at Terran, too afraid of seeing whatever was on his face. He bit his lip and took a deep breath.

"You must think I'm a fool," Micah said, his voice breaking.

"No," Terran said, and he gently lifted Micah's chin. "No, I do not. I think the world is cruel and unfair. I think that you were taken advantage of. I think that these men who call themselves civilized are truly monsters."

Micah wanted to look away, but he couldn't. Terran was holding him there, watching him carefully, and Micah couldn't deny the admiration and love in his gaze. It caught in his chest and bloomed.

"Thank you," Micah said. "Thank you for saving me and just for… everything. Thank you for showing me that it wouldn't always be like…like him."

Terran pulled Micah to him, pressing a kiss gently to his neck and holding him against his chest. They breathed there for a moment, and Micah tried not to cry again. Eventually Terran pulled back, his face deadly serious.

"If I ever meet Edwyn Patterson, he is going to wish that he was never born," Terran said, his voice its deepest, most resonant growl. "He had better stay far, far away from any forest if he wants to live."

Terran's fingers had drifted down and were resting almost reverently on the scars on Micah's neck. Micah wanted to pull back, to cover them again with his hand, but something in Terran's gaze stopped him. He carefully lifted his hand and wrapped it around Terran's fingers. He tried for a smile, but he was sure that it didn't meet his eyes.

"Please stay here," Terran said. "Please. Let me protect you, let me crown you in flowers. This world has taken too much from you, and from me. I want to be selfish, I don't want you to be taken from me too."

Micah squeezed his eyes shut. After a moment he said, "I need to stop Fenwick. I think I can, and it will be safe. I'll be safe."

"Micah, please," Terran begged, his voice on the edge of breaking.

"It's different here than last time," Micah said, pressing his forehead against Terran's. "I learned how to talk to people, I have friends. They know me in town. And nobody likes Fenwick. I'll be fine. And once it's taken care of, I'll come back. And…and I'll stay. I promise."

Terran pulled Micah to him and squeezed hard. Now that Micah knew just how strong Terran truly was, he was keenly aware how much he was holding back. He knew just how gentle Terran had been. He wrapped his arms around Terran and squeezed back, burying his face in Terran's steady, strong shoulder.

"Don't be long," Terran said. "And please, don't get hurt."

Micah nodded against his shoulder, and Terran helped him up. Whatever magic healing was found in the forest had definitely expedited the process of repairing his skin. As he stood, sticky, cool leaves that he hadn't noticed before fell from his arms, neck, chest, and legs, revealing burns that were already partially healed. He limped as he walked, the bruises still making him sore. Terran took his hand and soon they were at the edge of the forest not far from Roseyard.

Terran leaned down and kissed Micah, then said, "Please be right, I don't want you to be stolen. You are far too precious for that."

Micah smiled and said, "It'll be fine. I just can't let him keep getting away with this."

"Bring him into the forest and I'll solve the problem," Terran said, his voice low and dangerous.

Micah shook his head. "I want the town to know what he did."

"All right," Terran said. "You're a brave man, Micah. Brave and beautiful."

Micah felt himself grow hot, blushing at that. He looked up at Terran, whose face seemed to be stuck in some kind of debate. He finally smiled.

"I love you," he rumbled. He had already said it to Micah in a thousand other ways, but stated so plainly, so clearly, it was a promise. An oath. A guarantee that he would be there, waiting for Micah, no matter what trials he faced outside of the cool, safe forest. Micah felt as though he might cry, and he didn't understand why until he realized that no one had told him that since his mother's death more than a decade ago. And how long had it been for Terran?

"I love you, too," Micah said, hoping that his fire-weakened, broken, and sob-struck voice carried that same weight of promise. By the look in Terran's eyes, it did.

Terran pressed one last kiss to Micah's hair and then let him go. Micah stumbled towards Roseyard, limping on a bad leg, still struggling to breathe. He turned back to see Terran staring after him, gripping onto a tree, and he nodded at him that he would be fine. The further he got from the forest, the weaker he felt. He realized that he was still wearing the blood-stained, torn, scorched sleep clothes from the night before. He was barefoot and he was sure that his hair was soot-stained. Well, he would certainly cut a striking figure walking into town like this.

As he entered town, a crowd started to gather. He limped, and now that he was out of view of the forest, he touched his side over a likely broken rib, wincing. Murmuring people lined the streets, unsure of what to do until he tripped over a cobblestone and fell with a yelp to the ground. That spurred a few people to rush over to help him up, asking if he was okay.

Kay suddenly burst through the crowd and hurried up to him, a horrified look in her eyes as she examined his beaten and bruised body. She lifted his face and stared at him in shock, then started calling for the doctor.

"No," Micah said, his voice sounded even worse out here than in the forest. "I need…I need to report a crime. Can you take me to the townhead?"

Kay looked conflicted, but she said, "All right, yes, we'll get you there. What happened? Oh, Micah, whose blood is this?"

That was the wrong question to ask, because it was Wilbur's. The saltwater started to rise in his throat, and Kay dropped his face and hugged him despite the filth. Suddenly, another familiar face was beside hers, that of Henderson. He was looking flush and plump, but very concerned.

"By the stars, what happened, man?" Henderson asked, slipping his arm under Micah's shoulder and supporting him. "Mr. Harlow, this cannot stand, do you hear me? Let's get you to the townhead. Someone get the doctor! I'll pay, of course. Have her meet us at the hall. Now, I won't hear of it, Mr. Harlow. Someone get him some new clothes—I'll cover the cost! No protesting, Mr. Harlow."

Micah wasn't putting up much of a protest, if only because it was increasingly hard to speak. Another person, a woman whose children he had given free cookies to, ran up with a cup of cool water and held it up to his lips as Henderson and another lumberjack helped him to walk. Kay stayed close to him, chewing her bottom lip in worry.

There was a near-parade through Roseyard with Micah as its focus. That many people surrounding him brought back unpleasant flashes of Steephall, but there was a different energy to the crowd. After a bit, Henderson got one of his men to keep the crowd back, having seen how Micah's face twisted in fear. They eventually made it to the town hall, and without even asking, Kay burst into the townhead's office.

The townhead, a needle of a woman named Analisa Bracken, took one look at Micah and leapt up in horror.

"Heavens, has the doctor been called? What happened? Quick, get him a chair!" Bracken, quick and efficient, got her answers immediately. Yes, the doctor had been called. He stumbled into town looking like that, saying he needed to report a crime. Here was a chair.

The moment Micah sat, he realized just how tired he was. The healing of the forest had done wonders, but it hadn't been finished when he left. His pain was nearly unbearable. And he knew that the doctor, when she finally arrived, would want him to rest and he couldn't do that. Not with Fenwick on the loose.

The new clothes arrived before the doctor did and Henderson insisted on getting Micah washed and dressed immediately, but Micah knew that if he didn't speak now, he might never. He agreed to let them clean and change him as he spoke. A bowl of warm water and several rags were carried in and Kay peeled off his red-soaked shirt and started washing the blood and dirt and soot off of him without the slightest blush.

"What day is it?" Micah rasped.

When it was confirmed that it was, indeed, only the next day, Micah nodded solemnly. The room was filled with Bracken, Henderson, the lumberjack, the runner who got the clothes, and Kay. He took a deep shuddering breath.

"Would it be too much trouble if I could get some tea? Maybe with honey?" he asked.

"No, of course not," Bracken said, and she summoned a servant to fetch tea, then turned to Micah and asked, "Mr. Harlow, you said that you had a crime to report, and I can see that you are badly injured. Would you please elaborate?"

He told them everything that happened: the house fire, the hive being set ablaze, the hens having their necks snapped, and through tears, Wilbur's death. The tea arrived and he took steadying sips of it throughout his story. He told them that he was able to escape through the forest, which wasn't a lie, but he thought they might think him delusional if he told them about Terran.

"Did you recognize any of the men who attacked you?" Bracken asked.

By now, Kay had washed him, and he was dressed in new clothes.

They were far finer than what he had been wearing daily. The shirt was a soft cream and the cuffs and neck were embroidered with incredibly intricate floral designs; with the detail and the silken thread, they had to have cost a fortune. The pants were thick and sturdy—they wouldn't need mending every season—and they had even gotten him a pair of boots. Guilt at having such fine things ate at him, but he nodded to the townhead.

"Only one, ma'am," he said, his voice slightly stronger after the tea. "I know that you may not believe me, but it is true. He was the leader. He did not do anything to me directly, but he ordered everything that happened. It was Charles Fenwick."

The room grew icy, all eyes on him. It had apparently been a very long time since anyone had risked accusing Fenwick of any wrongdoing. Kay held his hand and squeezed. Henderson folded his arms and looked at the townhead, daring her to question Micah.

"This is a very serious accusation," Bracken said carefully. "Now, I'm going to send a few runners to confirm your story at your cottage—"

"What, was the state he was in when he got to town not proof enough?" Kay snapped at her.

"We're dealing with the law here, Miss Lindon," Bracken said. "We must be certain. But I need to ask you, Mr. Harlow, did you happen to hear any other names?"

Micah thought for a moment and then said, "Yes. Mr. Fenwick told a man named David to kill Wilbur. Er, my donkey."

"Could be David Harrison," Henderson said. "He runs around with Fenwick's crowd."

"We'll bring him in for questioning," Bracken said. "For now, Mr. Harlow will need a place to stay while we figure this out."

"Oh, I couldn't possibly—" Micah started to say, and was immediately shot down by everyone in the room.

At that moment, the doctor arrived. She took one look at Micah and scolded all of them for daring to listen to the injured man and letting him file a report before receiving care. He was bundled off and ended up in Henderson's house in a spare bedroom. It was his first time meeting Mrs. Henderson and she treated him like royalty.

As soon as the doctor was done poking and prodding him, he collapsed onto the bed. Oh, he was far more tired than he had realized. But he had enough awareness to ask for Kay. She came into the room and knelt at his bedside.

"I swear, Micah, if you ask me to eat your sin and it's the sin of imposing on our hospitality, you are going to have additional injuries to worry about," Kay said, gripping his hand.

"No, it's not that, though maybe I'll petition you for that later," Micah said, weakly smiling. Kay didn't find it funny.

"Micah, please, what do you need me to do?" she asked.

"Please don't think I'm imagining things," Micah said softly.

"Whatever it is, you can trust me," Kay said with a smile, adding, "Tell me."

Micah told her everything about Terran. From start to finish, ending with the previous night. He watched her carefully as he spoke, her disbelief shifting halfway through the story to stunned silence. It seemed she did believe him.

"He's waiting for me," Micah said. "I told him it would be fast, and I need him to know that I'm okay, and I'm still coming back."

Kay sat cross-legged on the ground and looked up at him before saying, "All right. Do you think he'll believe me?"

Micah closed his eyes, then said, "Tell him the message comes from his sweet."

"His '*sweet*'?"

Micah smiled and said simply, "It's his pet name for me. I don't know why. But it should be enough. If he still doesn't believe you, tell him I'm sorry that I lost the yellow ribbon."

Kay stared at him blinking for a moment before shaking her head and saying, "I guess I shouldn't be surprised. All right, yes. I'll tell him."

Kay got up and leaned down to gently squeeze Micah's shoulder.

Micah didn't stay awake much longer after the door closed behind her. At least this night, he didn't dream of much of anything.

IN THE MORNING, HE WOKE TO THE SMELL OF FRESHLY BAKED bread and something rich and meaty being cooked over a hot stove. He sat up and groaned. Every inch of him was sore and he was starving. He glanced at the door just in time to see it shut and hear the telltale giggles of a young girl running away. Moments later, the door flew open and all three of the Hendersons bustled in with a tray of tea, biscuits, and gravy. There was even a small dish of honey. Micah was a tad uncomfortable as the three of them sat and watched him eat, but Markus Henderson gave him the rundown on how the rest of the day had gone.

"Well, Mr. Fenwick is going to get what's coming to him," Henderson said, nodding sternly. "David Harrison was indeed very helpful. He had a broken arm, you know, and he was quite upset with Fenwick. He gave the names of the other men and confirmed that yes, indeed, Fenwick was there and behind it. Also, he's been behind many, many more, subtler incidents. Remember when Marion Beath's roof collapsed? That was him as well."

Micah nodded and said softly, "I thought so."

"There's a paper trail as long as a road. He's been buying up land and bullying those who wouldn't sell. This is the final straw, and they're going to arrest him." Henderson's eyes gleamed, and he punctuated each sentence by pounding his fist into his open hand.

Micah straightened and his eyes lit up. "They are?"

"As soon as they find him," Henderson said sheepishly. "The damnedest thing, no one knows where he went. The last time anyone saw him was the day before he attacked you."

"Oh," Micah said, fear creeping ivylike into his mind.

"Don't worry, though." Henderson said. "They'll find him soon enough. Until then, you're free to stay with us. You changed our goddamn lives. Saved my livelihood, saved our home, and the work for all my men. No wonder Fenwick hates you. Ouch! Sorry."

Henderson's wife had jabbed him hard in the side with her elbow, and she added gently, "Mr. Harlow, I apologize for my husband. You'll be safe, of course."

"I never said he wouldn't be safe!"

"You implied it!"

They bickered back and forth like, well, like an old married couple. Micah couldn't help but smile, laughing into his teacup, until a hand tugged on his sleeve. He looked down and saw the little Henderson girl staring up at him.

"I'm sorry about your donkey," she said. "I remember him from the market days."

"Thank you," Micah said, a sad smile on his face.

He wondered how much of the story had spread through town, and found out as he went for a slow, discouraged walk around Roseyard. People kept running up to him, asking after his well-being, offering their condolences, and thanking him. He had been right when he had said that no one liked Fenwick.

He didn't even realize where he was going until he ended up at Kay's house. He took a breath and then knocked. He heard coughing and movement within and Kay appeared at the door. She smiled softly and moved out onto the step.

"Sorry, my brother is having a bad day," she said. "If you want to talk, we can go to the square."

Micah smiled and nodded. Kay matched his snail's pace, and they moved slowly to the square. It was only a few blocks away, but it still took them a considerable amount of time to get there. When they arrived, they sat on a bench together and Micah closed his eyes. The cool spring breeze blew through his hair and against his skin.

"It's strange seeing you without the hat," Kay said softly.

"Fenwick threw it in the fire," Micah said. "It's gone."

Kay was quiet for a moment and then she said, "I'm sorry."

"It was just a hat," Micah said. After a moment, he added, "What did he say?"

"He believed me before I gave him any of the little code phrases," Kay said with a smirk. "Apparently you've told him about me. But he wanted me to tell him what you had said anyway. He says that you're much prettier than the ribbon."

Micah laughed sadly and said, "He would."

"He wishes you would come now," Kay said. "But he understands why you can't. He said to tell you to be safe. And that he would love to rip Fenwick in two."

Micah buried his face in his hands and laughed.

"You're not coming back after you go into the woods again, are you?" Kay asked.

Micah was silent and then he said, "Probably not. I fit better there, anyway. I seem to always ruin things with people. I think I might be cursed."

Kay snorted and said, "You cannot be serious."

Micah gave her a strange look and said, "I am. You don't know… what I did before."

"Yeah, you won't tell me," Kay said, rolling her eyes. "If I know anything about you, it wasn't your fault but you're blaming yourself. Like how I can tell you're blaming yourself for Wilbur and the hens and the bees when you were outnumbered, what, ten to one? And, I hate to say it, you're a twig of a man and you *were* nearly snapped in two."

Staring down at his hands, Micah asked, "You still owe me a sin-eating, right?"

Kay furrowed her brow and said, "You're cashing that in? Now?"

Micah nodded.

"All right," Kay said, and then bit her lip. "You know that I'll see what happened, right? When I eat it. Are you all right with that?"

"That's why I'm asking for it," Micah said, closing his eyes. "I want to tell you, but I don't think I can get my mouth to work for me."

Kay nodded. She took him by the shoulders and turned him towards her. Placing her hand firmly on his chest and closing her eyes, she muttered strange words under her breath.

There was a sharp pain in his chest then, a twang against his heart. He gasped and the memories of Steephall flashed through his mind. He had avoided those memories so well, but for the second time in as many days, they swarmed him. He nearly buckled as she pulled the wriggling black mass from him.

Oh. It was much smaller than he thought. He was imagining the size of a great snake, something that could wrap around his entire body, but this was barely the size of an earthworm. It squirmed between Kay's fingers.

"You thought it was going to be bigger, right?" Kay asked.

Micah nodded.

"It's always that way," Kay said, sighing. "The people expecting it to be small have huge sins, the ones expecting it to be huge, itty bitty. Down the hatch."

She opened her mouth and placed it on her tongue. It wiggled until she closed her mouth and swallowed. After a moment, she looked at Micah. It was strange. Micah could still remember everything that happened in Steephall, but it wasn't shackling him down anymore. He could see it more clearly now and look at it without guilt or pain.

"Huh," Kay said. "Fuck that guy."

Micah couldn't help it. He burst out laughing. He laughed so hard that it started a coughing fit that sent tears streaming down his face. Kay rubbed circles into his back and sighed, smiling softly.

9

THE SWORD

THREE DAYS AFTER MICAH STUMBLED INTO TOWN, BEATEN AND bloody, they still hadn't found Fenwick. Henderson was appalled and made it loudly known as he strode about the house ranting about the incompetence of the town guard. His wife Sara would cross her arms and shake her head in agreement.

They had searched Fenwick's house and had indeed found paperwork and plans. The bruisers who hadn't fled had confessed to nearly everything. All this was relayed to Micah by Kay as she came to visit him. The doctor, appalled that Micah had gone for a walk in his condition, forbade him from leaving the house again, much to his annoyance.

After exactly one day of lying in bed, Micah had tried desperately to make himself useful in the Henderson household. He kept getting shooed away from chores by Sara and laughed at by the little girl, Paisley, because of it. Sara caught him washing dishes and about had a heart attack, grabbing him by the elbows and literally pushing him out of the kitchen, all while lecturing him about how guests weren't responsible for housework, especially not in his state.

Eventually, he went to sit out in the garden, eyes closed, letting the wind blow through his hair. The Hendersons were in the process of buying him a whole new wardrobe despite his protests. He had four new shirts, all as stunningly beautiful as the first one, two fine pairs of trousers, and plenty of socks to wear under the new boots. When Paisley came up to him with a new straw hat, it took everything in him not to start crying. He smiled at her and put it on. Admittedly, it fit much better than his old one.

He watched lazy honey bees buzz around the flowers, a sad yearning deep in his chest, a sorrow for what he had lost. And, watching the people on the street, he thought about what he would lose when he went with Terran. He knew, in his deepest heart of hearts, that by Terran's side was where he wanted to be, but still. He would miss the simple joys of being, well, human.

At the end of the third day, with still no sign of Fenwick, Micah decided that he would go and give Terran an update himself. It was nearing sunset, but it would be fine. The forest would be safe for him, so he let the Hendersons know that he would be back later. When he saw Kay in the street she told him it was a bad idea, but nevertheless, he went.

As he got closer to the tree line, he seemed already to be able to breathe easily. Birdsong filled his ears and the rich, sweet air cooled his lungs rather than burning them. His limp lessened, his tender skin stopped aching. Yes, this was where he belonged. He got to the tree line, placed his hand on an oak, and smiled.

"Terran?" he asked into the air.

There was no response. Instead, an eerie breeze blew through the branches. What had felt so comforting just moments ago now had a sinister edge to it, a dark bite. Something felt wrong. Oh no. Was Terran angry with him? Micah supposed he deserved that; he hadn't been back to speak with him since the night of the attack. Terran might think that he had abandoned him.

"Terran?" Micah called, a bit more desperately. Then he felt something cold and sharp against his scarred throat.

"So that's the name of the monster that helped you escape,

warlock," Fenwick's low voice said in his ear. "If you move without my say-so, if you speak without my permission, I need you to understand that I will slit your pretty little throat, and unlike Edwyn Patterson, I have no qualms about using all of your lifeblood to water the grass. Do you understand?"

"Yes," Micah whispered.

"We're going into the forest now, and you're going to take me to the center, wherever the beast sleeps," Fenwick growled, low and angry. "I know you know where it is, I know that you're the beast's little whore, warlock."

"I won't take you," Micah said, his voice firm.

He heard Fenwick growl in response and felt the blade more firmly against his throat. But he noticed just the slightest bit of hesitation. Micah gritted his teeth and tried his luck.

"Go ahead, then, kill me," Micah said, and he felt the pressure on the blade lessen just the smallest amount.

Micah took the opportunity to look back at Fenwick. The man was angry and disheveled, his formerly slicked-back hair in total disarray and his fine clothes rumpled and soiled. His face was twisted into a sneer. The blade against Micah's throat was not a dagger, as he had thought, but a sword. Unfortunately, Fenwick held it as though he knew what he was doing.

"I don't think that you want that, warlock," Fenwick said, eyes rolling wildly. "You may not value your own life, but what will happen to the people who call you friend? Miss Lindon, whom you have so thoroughly entranced, Mr. Henderson, who seems to believe that you are his own personal savior, or even your forest beast. Lead on, warlock."

Micah swallowed, his scars scraping ever so slightly against the blade pressed to his throat. Fenwick nudged his shoulder and Micah, gritting his teeth, stepped through the tree line.

It was dark within the forest now. Unlike during his other visits, the trees did not welcome him like an old friend. He still knew the way, but it was going to take a while. Micah was watching the ground, trying not to stumble and fall directly into the blade against his neck. Fenwick's breathing was heavy behind him, directly in his ear. He once again swallowed and decided that Fenwick needed him, so it would be safe enough to ask questions.

"What is your plan, Fenwick?" Micah asked.

"Dropped the 'mister,' eh?" Fenwick said, and exhaled quickly. "I'm going to destroy this forest from the core. You're probably wondering why your beast hasn't come to your rescue, eh?"

"It had crossed my mind," Micah said flatly, trying to hide the shake in his voice.

"Your little friend Patterson was very helpful," Fenwick said. "Researched all sorts of ways to deal with warlocks like you. And those also apply to spirits, you know. Cold iron, like the dagger he used on your neck. All sorts of wards. I hadn't put much stock in them when I first read his letters, I admit, but after your display back on your land…well…"

"I'm not a warlock," Micah said, not able to hide the fear in his voice anymore.

Fenwick laughed and said, "Sure! And I'm not about to achieve my family's dream. I do think, Mr. Harlow, if you survive this, I'm going to ship you back to Steephall. Let Patterson decide what to do with you. How does that sound?"

Fear twisted inside Micah. He never, never wanted to see Edwyn again. And the people of Steephall would certainly not welcome him. What would Edwyn do to him if he had him again? Micah fisted his hands to stop them shaking and thought of Terran's steady hands and voice, his promise that nothing would hurt him again, and found the peace that he needed.

"This isn't going to work," Micah said.

"You keep telling yourself that," Fenwick said with a smirk in his voice. "I'm sure it's a great comfort."

Micah was silent after that. It was dark and hard to see. Micah tried to mislead Fenwick, taking him down long winding paths in the wrong direction. Fenwick caught on the third time he did it and grabbed Micah's hand, taking his pinky finger and snapping the bone with ease. Micah screamed and Fenwick clapped his hand over Micah's mouth, stinging his skin. Micah didn't try that again.

It must have been near midnight when the familiar feel of the center of the forest sank into Micah's skin. The tone of the birdsong deepened, and the air became richer, fuller. A gentle light, magical, surrounded them. Micah tensed. He needed to figure out a way to throw off Fenwick, to stop him. Fenwick's grip on his shoulder tightened, the blade pressed harder.

"Call him," Fenwick whispered in his ear.

Micah closed his eyes. Once again, he would be the reason that something was destroyed, because he dared to have just a bit of joy, just a bit of happiness for himself. Why was he like this? He really was cursed. He bit down on his inner cheek and swallowed.

"Terran?" he asked as tears started to flow.

"Micah?" The voice came immediately. "Oh, I didn't feel when you entered the forest! I'm glad you're here! Did they finally find the son of a bitch? I would love to—"

Terran came into view and his wide smile immediately vanished, replaced by a look of such unrestrained anger that Micah flinched. His eyes locked onto Fenwick, just behind Micah. The transformation started immediately, Terran's antlers sharpening, his fingernails becoming long claws, his snarl filling with sharp teeth.

"Terran, I'm so sorry," Micah said through his tears. He was crying so much these days. "I tried, I am so sorry."

Terran's eyes flicked to Micah and he rumbled out, "You, my sweet, have nothing to apologize for. He, however, is about to see what happens when he hurts the man I love."

Micah felt the sword press even harder on his throat as Fenwick said, "Careful, beast. If you want your little warlock to still be breathing at the end of this, you'll not touch a hair on my head."

"Don't let him do whatever he's planning, Terran" Micah said. "It's okay. You made me happy for a bit, it's okay."

"'Tis not okay," Terran roared, his voice shaking the trees. "No, Micah. I'm being selfish. I want you."

Micah's breath hitched and he said, "Terran…Terran, he's going to destroy everything. I'm not worth that."

"You are," Terran said, his eyes now locked on Micah's. "You are worth that."

"This is all very sweet," Fenwick said, shoving Micah forward as he walked, making Terran tense. "But I'm here for a reason and it's not to watch melodrama. Now, where is the tree?"

"How did you know about that?" Micah snapped. "I didn't tell you anything!"

With a wicked smile in his voice, Fenwick said, "Helpful letters."

Terran stood rigid, practically growling, as Fenwick moved into the grove with Micah in front of him like a shield. Micah's mind was racing, running through a thousand different things that might let him escape this, might stop Fenwick. As Fenwick saw the yew tree at the center where he and Terran had spent a few wonderful nights together, where Terran had tended Micah's wounds, Micah felt Fenwick's grip relax ever so slightly.

"There it is, just as it should be," Fenwick said.

"What are you going to do?" Micah asked, a plan starting to form.

"I'm going to stab this iron sword directly into the heartwood," Fenwick said. "It'll kill the forest. I'll clear it, it'll be my land to do with as I please. I will become everything I want to be, I'll have the power, the money—"

He didn't get to finish the sentence, because Micah, with Fenwick's grip now loose, had leaned forward, then brought his head back directly into Fenwick's nose with a sickening smash. His new straw hat fell back, blinding Fenwick for a moment. The back of Micah's skull ached, but it was worth it as blood gushed from Fenwick's nose onto his back. As Fenwick cursed and pulled Micah's hat out of his face, his sword hand dropped and Micah broke out of his grip.

Micah was gasping, but he yelled, "Terran!"

Fenwick only had a second to react, because Terran was racing out of the trees. Without Micah there, there was nothing to keep the spirit back. Micah scrambled out of the way until he felt the steady, sturdy bark of the yew behind him. He watched as Terran tackled Fenwick, the two men wrestling on the ground in a flurry of movement. But it wasn't like the way Terran had attacked the men a few nights ago; something was wrong. His powerful blows were being deflected. A hit that should have torn Fenwick asunder became the powerful blow of a normal man. Fenwick's wards were protecting him, and Terran howled in frustration, still trying to attack the monstrous, wolflike man.

Fenwick, for his part, was swinging the sword wildly at Terran, but Terran was fast. He dove swiftly out of the way of every blow. Fenwick's eyes had gained their predatory gleam, and they carefully watched this prince of the forest dance. It was a stalemate. Micah was sitting against the yew catching his breath when he saw it. The key to ending this, giving Terran the upper hand. There was a glint against Fenwick's chest that hadn't been there before. A pendant that had fallen out of Fenwick's shirt during the struggle with Terran. It looked like iron.

Micah pulled himself up onto unsteady legs and waited for an opening. That was a mistake, because Terran's attention was drawn to him and Fenwick was able to hit Terran's arm, spraying the ground with blood. Terran hissed and stepped back while Fenwick laughed. Micah gritted his teeth and rushed forward.

He ducked, unskillfully but well enough to avoid being hit, under Fenwick's guard and grabbed at the necklace. Fenwick only had a moment to realize what was happening before Micah pulled roughly and with all his strength on the pendant, snapping the cord. Micah cheered in triumph and scrambled back, throwing the ward into the weeds at the edge of the grove.

"Now, Terran! He's not protected anymore!" Micah shouted, looking towards the spirit, but then pain exploded in his belly.

He looked down to see the hilt of the sword protruding from his abdomen, red soaking up through his shirt. He sputtered and stepped back, then looked up to see Fenwick smirking in triumph and anger. Micah wrapped his hands around the hilt and coughed, blood exploding from his mouth.

"Well, that is unfortunate, isn't it, Mr. Harlow? All of this could have been so easily avoided had you just sold me your land at the start," Fenwick said, stepping back and sneering at him. "Now, if you'll excuse me—"

Fenwick didn't get a chance to finish whatever he was going to say. Terran was upon him. More than that, the entire forest exploded. From below Fenwick's feet, roots burst out of the ground, wrapping around his legs, then torso, then neck and arms, holding him in place. Birds swooped down, gouging his skin. Thistles, stinging nettles, and deadly nightshade all started creeping up his body, digging into his open wounds.

All that would have been enough to end Fenwick where he stood, but it was Terran who, with clawed fingers and sharp teeth, tore him apart. Roots pulled what was left of the man deep into the forest floor. All he was able to do before he died was look at Micah and make gurgling noises that could have been words, or perhaps just the sounds of the pain he had inflicted on so many others coming back to him threefold.

Micah, in the meantime, grasped the hilt of the sword and drew it out of his belly as though he were unsheathing it. He threw it aside, and it sank into the earth like Fenwick had. However, that was a dire mistake. As soon as the wound was unstopped, his lifeblood gushed out, soaking the ground and turning it red. Micah didn't last on his feet long and fell to the ground, making pained gurgling sounds of his own.

"Micah!" Terran had rushed over, and his beautiful face was all that Micah could see with his blurring vision.

"Oh, hello, love," Micah said between pained gasps. "Fenwick is dead, that's good."

"He is, he is," Terran said, his hands pressing down on the cavern in Micah's belly, trying and failing to stop the bleeding.

"That's good," Micah repeated, closing his eyes and letting stars dance on his eyelids. "He won't be able to hurt anyone else."

"Open your eyes, my sweet," Terran said, his voice cracking. "Don't go to sleep, not yet."

It was a monumental task, but Micah did it. He peeled his eyes open to see Terran's, full of tears, looking down at him with so much sadness. Micah was very cold and shaky, but he cupped Terran's face gently with his hand.

"Don't be sad," Micah said. "Don't cry, I do that. You're the stoic one."

Terran laughed, and the tears brimming at the corners of his eyes spilled over, falling onto Micah. Micah smiled at him, the world as icy cold as the middle of winter, though he knew that the grove with the yew always had the pleasant warmth of a spring day. Oh. He was dying. He breathed deeply.

"Thank you, Terran," Micah said, his tongue tripping over each word.

"Micah, why are you thanking me?" Terran asked, his voice breaking on a sob. "You're dying because of me. My sweet, my sweet..."

Terran gave up on pushing on the wound and picked up Micah's body, grown impossibly limp, and held him to his chest. Terran's warmth seeped a bit into Micah's skin, and Micah lifted an arm around Terran with an impossible effort.

"You loved me, even with the way I am, how I destroy everything I touch," Micah said, his voice surprisingly even and firm. "Even though I'm cursed."

Terran pulled Micah back, holding him in his gaze as he said, "Micah. You're not cursed, you're a blessing. You're easy to love."

At those words, Micah broke into a smile and closed his eyes. He could hear Terran repeating his name, over and over, begging him to stay. Micah was so very, very tired. Stars danced in his vision as, one by one, each sense left him. He couldn't smell the forest or taste the air. The stars faded from his vision, leaving him in darkness, and he lost the sensation of Terran holding him. The last thing to leave him was Terran's voice, mixed with birdsong, calling his name. Then, there was nothing.

10

THE FLOWER

THEN THERE WAS SOMETHING. A VOICE, AGAIN, THROUGH THE dark. It wasn't one he recognized. It hardly sounded like a single voice at all. It was the voice of his mother, the voice of Terran, of Henderson, of Kay, of Marion, even, terrifyingly, of Edwyn and Fenwick. It was a blend of the voices of every person who had touched his life, joined into a cacophonous melody.

"What to do with you?" the voice, the voices, said.

"Pardon?" Micah asked. He was just a voice as well. He couldn't feel his body or, well, anything at all.

"You saved us," the voices said. "The sword that was meant for our heart, you took instead."

"What?" Micah said, and if he had a body, he would have shaken his head. "Wait, who are you?"

"Perhaps a better question would be what are we?" the voices said. "But we think you already know."

After a moment, Micah ventured, "The forest?"

"Indeed, we're just borrowing voices," they replied.

"Oh," Micah said. "I'm glad that you're okay. Is Terran all right?"

"His bodily injuries will heal, have already healed," the forest said.

122

"But the other injuries will take a long time. He will be sad and quite lonely again."

"That's my fault," Micah said immediately. "I just...I can't do anything right."

"No, you can," the forest said. "Without your intervention, the cruel man would have destroyed us and our guardian."

"Without my intervention, he would have never been there in the first place," Micah said flatly.

"He would have destroyed us eventually by more mundane means, we are sure," the forest said. "And you stopped that. Even when it would have been easy to disappear, to let it go, you stopped him."

Micah had no response to that, so he said nothing. If he had a body in this strange space, he would have curled in on himself, would have squeezed his eyes shut, but he was left exposed to his own thoughts, unable to hide from them.

"We would like to thank you," the voices said. Hearing this from the combination of voices was uncanny and Micah felt even more unmoored.

"You...you don't have to," Micah said. "Anyone would have done it."

"No, they would not," the forest said, simply, as though it were saying the sun existed in the sky.

"Well, you are welcome, I suppose," Micah said, not knowing what else to say.

Whispering exploded around him. Some of it sounded like discussion, some of it like hot debate, but the voices slowly coalesced again.

"We would like to offer you a boon," the forest said.

Micah wished he had eyes to blink in surprise, but no such luck, so he hesitantly asked, "A boon?"

"Our guardian is begging for it regardless," the forest said and then, in an almost giddy voice, added, "We've never heard of having two guardians, but it would be fun to be the first."

"What?" Micah asked, his voice soft with disbelief.

"You've certainly proven that you'll lay your life down for the forest, for all the creatures that live within, Micah Harlow," the voices said. "Why not? You can be given strength and life and a purpose here. And you will be able to stay with our guardian."

Micah was shocked. He had been sure, once he had pulled out the sword and his blood gushed out, that it was the end. He took a moment to collect the thoughts that were ambushing him and tried to relax.

"All right. All right," Micah said, a laugh exploding out of him. "Just…I have a question."

"Of course," the forest said. "What is it?"

"I'll have to stay in the borders of the forest forever, yes?" Micah asked.

"About that," the forest said, and they seemed oddly happy. "We have an idea."

As they laid out their plan, Micah smiled, even without a mouth.

Micah's eyes flew open as he gasped for air. The sweet air of the forest, the rich scent of the yew and the flowers that grew around it, flooded into him. He blinked. The light seemed…different. Motes of dust danced in the air, refracting the sunlight and mesmerizing him with their sparkle. He lifted a hand carefully and pushed them around, giggling to himself as he did so.

What was going on? He hardly remembered. He remembered being cold…very cold…and then it came flooding back to him. His hand shot to his stomach where the sword had been only to find smooth skin. Not even a scar. He blinked and looked down at the pink skin, fresh and clear as a baby's, in utter confusion. Then another odd thing occurred to him. He was naked. A blush crept up his neck and he lifted himself up from among the roots of the yew and looked around to see if anyone was near.

When he braced a hand on one of the protruding roots, he yelped in surprise because wildflowers exploded from where his fingertips touched the bark. He curled his hand into a fist and stared, dumbstruck, at the blooms. He breathed in, pulling his legs up to his chest, to preserve his decency if nothing else, and looked around. The little grove was empty. The wind blew slowly through the branches of the yew, rustling the leaves, and birdsong filled the little clearing, somehow even more alive and beautiful now than ever. Micah breathed out. And then, in a moment of silly vanity, he reached up and felt his throat. Those scars were still there. He sighed.

Then a twig snapped quietly, something he wouldn't have heard before, but his ears were so much more sensitive now. His head snapped over towards the sound. Something was coming closer to the grove. He pulled himself inward and scrunched up against the tree, the rough bark biting into his bare back. He lowered himself so that whatever was coming wouldn't be able to see him, but he'd be able to see it.

Out of the tree line, moments later, burst Terran. He looked rough, leaves and twigs tangled in his hair and beard, deep purple bruises under his eyes, and his eyes themselves…oh. Micah had never seen them so sad, so void of the life and joy that he had seen there so many times. Despite his current state, Micah had to let him know that he was alive, that he was there. He sat up and, looking over at Terran, smiled.

"Terran?" he called.

Terran's head shot up and he bounded over to Micah, who barely had time to react before Terran was picking him up, squeezing him to his chest, and swinging him around, laughing through tears. Micah wrapped his arms around Terran and squeezed back. It was several minutes before Terran set him down, then held the back of his head and started kissing him furiously. On the mouth, yes, but he peppered his face with small little kisses, each freckle graced by his lips until Micah was laughing uncontrollably as Terran's beard tickled his skin. It wasn't until Micah held Terran's face in his hands and pulled back to press their foreheads together that Terran stopped.

"You're alive," Terran said, his voice breaking.

"Something like that," Micah said, laughing, but he could feel tears forming in the corners of his eyes.

"I thought I had lost you, my sweet," Terran said, looking down into Micah's face with such relief that it tore Micah's heart in two.

"I know, I know," Micah said, losing the fight against his tears and cursing himself. "I'm sorry."

"Nothing to apologize for," Terran said. "Micah, I'm just so glad… what's this?"

Terran had been running his thumbs against Micah's cheeks, twining his fingers through Micah's blond curls, then brushing against Micah's ears. Micah's ears, which were now long and pointed like his. Micah shrugged with a smile as Terran's eyes lit up and he started to look over the rest of Micah.

"And you're not wearing any clothes," Terran said, eyes widening, and then broke away. "Hold on, hold on."

Micah laughed, and as Terran disappeared, he went back to sitting against the yew tree, bringing his knees up again and smiling to himself. He pushed his fingers into the ground and watched wildflowers spring up, rippling out from him like a wave. He blinked, watching them, and then he withdrew his fingers and they stopped. He smiled and Terran came back, a bundle of clothes in his hands, and looked at the flowers in awe.

"Was that you?" he asked, crouching down next to him.

"Yes," Micah said, looking down at his hands. "Yes, I think it was."

"Incredible," Terran said, looking at his face as though he were the most beautiful thing in the world. "Oh, but here. They are probably a bit too large, but they will work for now."

They were, indeed, too large. Micah was swimming in the large, old-fashioned tunic that continually fell off his shoulder. The trousers only stayed up because they had a cloth strap that could be tied up nice and tight. They couldn't stop laughing the first time Micah pulled them on, only to have them immediately fall to the ground in a puddle.

"You're here, though," Terran said. "And you're going to stay?"

Micah nodded and took Terran's hand in his, pressing a kiss to his knuckles, and said, "I am. The forest offered me this as thanks for, well…"

"Dying to protect it?" Terran said, his face growing serious.

"Yes, I suppose," Micah said, offering up a smile. "But I think it was worth it. Because you're here. And I'm still here, love."

Terran wrapped his arms around Micah, squeezing him like he'd never let him go. Micah held onto Terran's shoulders and they breathed together, there at the center of the forest. When they finally parted, Terran took Micah's arm in his hands and examined it. For the first time, Micah really, truly looked too.

They were like tattoos, except they moved. Beautiful depictions of flowers bloomed up and down both Micah's arms. Terran traced the ever-blooming, ever-changing blossoms with a finger and smirked at Micah. Before Micah could ask why, Terran reached out and plucked a small, pink flower from Micah's hair and offered it to him.

"You're a regular garden, my sweet," Terran said. "What gift did the forest give?"

"Wherever the bees fly, I may walk," Micah repeated, a smile playing on his lips. "I guess it makes sense, bees do love flowers."

"They do," Terran said. "I love flowers, too, y'know."

Micah laughed then, and after a moment he quietly added, "It also means that I can leave the forest, as long as there are bees."

"Oh," Terran said, and then a grin spread across his face. "Oh, you can go and see your friends! You can get revenge on that man in your old village!"

Micah smiled and said, "Yes to the first one, but only to say goodbye. As for Edwyn, I think I'll be happiest if I never see him again."

"All right," Terran said. "All right, but if he chooses to come in here…"

"I'll let you deal with him, love," Micah said, and he burst into joyful laughter at Terran's immense grin.

They spent the next few days together, Terran excitedly reintroducing him to everything in the forest now that his senses were exploding. Terran also could not keep his hands off of Micah. Whether it was peppering him with kisses, holding his hand, or even picking him up and holding him to his chest, it was as though Terran was afraid that someone would rip Micah away from him. Micah supposed he couldn't really blame him, and being so clearly wanted was very, very nice.

As he walked the forest, bees started to gather around him, lazily buzzing around the flowers blooming on his arms or where he rested his fingers. He noticed that if he was very happy, and not paying close attention, wildflowers would spring up around his feet. He would hold up a finger and a bee would happily land on it, crawling around and buzzing cheerfully.

Sometimes, Micah would gleefully hold it up to Terran, saying, "Look at her! Isn't she beautiful?"

Terran would grin and make some comment about how the bee paled in comparison to Micah. Once or twice, Terran would move to kiss Micah on the cheek only to press his lips to a bee that was resting there. Terran would huff in annoyance while Micah fought back a laugh.

Eventually, Micah decided that he needed to go into town to tell the townsfolk what had happened and to say goodbye. He stood at the tree line, Terran's arms wrapped loosely around his waist from behind. Micah's heart was pounding, nerves thudding. Terran's face was buried in his curls. Micah was only slightly annoyed that his hat was no longer comfortable with his new long ears, especially since now his hair seemed to be sprouting flowers.

"You'll be okay, right?" Terran said into his hair.

"I will," Micah said. "Fenwick is gone, and I'm just going to say goodbye. After all, if they really want to visit me, they can come to the forest."

"Don't be long," Terran said, hugging Micah to him one more time. "And don't bring back any more monsters."

Micah laughed, then turned around, pressing a kiss to Terran's scruffy cheek before saying, "I can promise you that."

He left Terran's arms and started moving outside of the forest. Fear wrapped its claws around Micah's heart, stopping his feet as he moved into the open air. It seemed to whisper to him. *If you leave now, you'll never come back, you'll abandon Terran, they'll trap you and never let you go.* But then a bee buzzed past his ear, landed on his arm, then crawled along the petals of a forget-me-not painted on his skin. He smiled, then continued on his way.

Once he got to the cobblestones of Roseyard, he glanced back to the forest and reddened in embarrassment. He had left a trail of wildflowers through the fields that led up to the town. The bees around him buzzed happily and he just shook his head with a smile. He had forgotten, honestly, that his feet were bare until there were hard stones underneath them. He stumbled a bit, missing the feeling of life radiating from the soles of his feet. He felt its cold absence once he wasn't touching the earth.

When he looked into the town, he was delighted to see booths and tents, people milling around and exchanging coin, chatting happily in the square. A market day. As he walked past small houses, those with window boxes or gardens exploded with life. People in their yards jumped in surprise and then looked at him in awe. Bees were flying around him, and his breath was catching in his throat as he moved through the street. People were starting to notice him, much like when he had come in, beaten and bloodied, after the fire, but the shock on their faces was of a different flavor.

"Micah Harlow?" a familiar voice called. "Micah, is that…is that you?"

He turned to see Kay standing there, a hand to her chest, a confused, hesitant look on her face. She stepped carefully towards him, cocking her head and squinting her eyes, looking at him in wonder.

"There's something different about you," she said, brow furrowing.

"Yes," Micah said. "There is."

A small crowd had gathered around them, booths and boards abandoned, hands dropped to their sides, whispers moving through the mass. He saw them all, recognized them. Some he knew well, others barely at all, but there they were.

"Well, what is it?" Kay asked. "I can't…I can't put my finger on it."

Bees buzzed excitedly around Micah as he smiled and said, "I'm not here for long, I'm going to go back to the forest soon. I don't belong here anymore."

"Oh pish!" Henderson's voice called from the side. "Of course you do, my boy! And we'll need you when Fenwick comes back."

Micah held up a finger and a bee landed on it as he said, "Fenwick isn't coming back. He…well, I know this sounds impossible, but he killed me."

Kay's eyes widened in shock, and murmurs rippled through the crowd, but they weren't of disbelief. It was the snap of understanding, the last piece coming into place, making the picture clear. They saw that Micah wasn't human anymore.

"Oh," Kay said, then gingerly stepped towards him. "What happened?"

"He tried to kill the forest," Micah said. "I got in the way. I died, then he died, and then the forest…well, it turned me into one of its guardians. I just came back…just this once to say goodbye, and thank you."

Kay took his hands, lifting them and turning them, before nodding solemnly, then wrapping Micah in a hug. Micah was surprised for only a moment before he returned it. Soon others came up to hug him, pat him on the back, shake his hand, all while bees buzzed peacefully around him.

"Now," Henderson said when it was his turn, "those are not the clothes my lovely wife had been picking out for you."

Micah laughed and said, "Unfortunately, the clothes I had been wearing got ruined by a sword tearing a hole through them and my blood staining them."

"Quite," Henderson said. "But these hardly fit you! Don't leave before we give you some proper clothes."

"Oh, and let us get you some bread! You won't find that in the forest," a voice called.

"And some blankets!"

"Oh, would you like some candy?"

"Milk! Milk, of course!"

"And cheese!"

Micah was stunned for only a moment, then he grinned at Henderson and said, "Well, you of all people know how to offer things to the guardian spirit of the forest."

"I do?" Henderson said, and then realization struck him. "I do! Yes, of course! I'll teach them all, I won't let them forget."

"Thank you," Micah said, his cheeks hurting from how hard he smiled.

Hours later, Micah was pulling himself from the town, back to the path of wildflowers he had left behind, when Kay rushed up and grabbed his wrist. He turned back to her, and he couldn't quite parse the look on her face.

"I don't…" Kay said, and her voice broke before she forced herself to continue. "I don't know how to thank you. You changed this whole town, and you gave up everything for it. We don't…we didn't… deserve you. I know you think that you ruin everything you touch, or at least you thought you did, but it isn't true. You get steeped in endless buckets of pain and yet you still give, you still are kind, and I'm just…I'm glad that you've found happiness."

Micah smiled at her and wrapped her in a hug. They stayed there for a moment, until she broke away wiping her eyes.

"I'll leave offerings in the forest until I'm too old to make the trek, and then I'll make the village kids do it, or whoever," Kay said. "You won't ever be forgotten, I want you to know that."

"And I won't forget you either," Micah said. "I promise."

Kay smiled at him, and he nodded back at her. Then he strode through the path of wildflowers, which all bloomed furiously around his feet. The sun was high in the sky over Roseyard and the forest beside it, and Micah couldn't be happier.

The trees welcomed Micah Harlow like welcoming a long-lost child home. It was a brisk spring afternoon after a lifetime of strife and chaos. As he walked into the trees, and into the arms of the spirit lurking there, bees buzzed and flowers bloomed, the wind shook the leaves in the branches of the trees, and birdsong filled the air. Terran swung him around as they moved through the forest, tending to a thousand little things, an eternity of life and love ahead of them.

ACKNOWLEDGMENTS

This book would not have been possible without the support of some very important people! First of all, my sister, who is a constant source of encouragement when it comes to my writing. Driving to the Renaissance Faire with you and forcing my book playlist upon you, I must be forever grateful.

Next, of course, my friends. We've spent years playing Dungeons & Dragons together, and I always appreciated being able to bounce ideas off y'all, as well as having you be my cheerleaders. I would especially like to thank my beta readers, who gave me such great feedback and helped me so much! Keiran Sage, Leaf, Dominoes, and clever.jpeg — you all are so wonderful and I am thankful for you reading the book early on and helping me craft it into the story it is now!

Also, I would like to thank my editor, Chris Zable. She was so incredibly helpful with making my book what it is now! Her feedback and corrections were so appreciated and I couldn't have done it without her.

I would also like to thank my cover artist, Eleonora North. Their beautiful work brought the story to life, and I am absolutely in love with the cover that they created.

ABOUT THE AUTHOR

Alex Larkspur is a lover of fantasy books of all kinds, but especially queer fantasy. They live in Texas with their dogs. There, you can usually find them hanging out in the library, playing Tabletop Role-Playing Games, or wandering museums when they aren't reading on the couch.

You can find them online @applesncinnamon.bsky.social

www.ingramcontent.com/pod-product-compliance
Lightning Source LLC
Chambersburg PA
CBHW070325120726
47909CB00008B/2607